WEARING SHADOWS

WEARING HORROR BOOK 2

SIMON PAUL WOODWARD

First published in Great Britain, the USA and Europe
by musingMonster Books, London in May 2021.

 Created with Vellum

For Tracy, again, with all my love and a bit more.

CONTENTS

WEARING SHADOWS

Cautiously, the young woman pushes open the door, peering into the hospital corridor beyond. It appears to be empty. A single strip light flickers at the far end. Shadows bloom and fade. Her breath comes in gasps as if she has been running. She hesitates. Lank blonde hair snakes across her brow and cheeks. She leans forwards, glancing left and right, sees a gurney angled across the corridor, its restraint straps hanging loose. Blood drips from its sides, tap, tap, tapping onto the floor in a spreading pool. Smeared, bloody footprints lead away from the gurney towards a set of swing doors at the far end of the corridor. She slips through the door. It closes behind her with a sucking sound and a click.

"Jason?" she says and waits for a response that does not come. She repeats his name, this time louder, almost shouting. "Jason?"

Blood is splattered across her white T-shirt. Scratches and grazes mark her tanned legs between her day-glo trainers and cut-off jean shorts. She edges forward, her body taut with tension. She glances at her shadow, watching it jerk into life, elongated and writhing, with each pulse from the faulty strip light.

She moves along the corridor. She's a big-eyed fawn sensing the attention of an unseen predator, ready to bolt at the first noise. She glances at her shadow again and grimaces. A few steps towards the gurney, following the trail of blood, staccato movement beneath the flickering light. Her shadow dances. Her eyes dart to it again.

"Cut! For fuck's sake, cut."

Mo Farzi, the film's director, lurches out from behind his monitor.

The illusion is broken. Kitty releases the tension she's been holding in her body while in character, rolls her shoulders, straightens her stance. Watches her shadow lengthen as she stands tall. She raises an eyebrow questioningly, as Mo stalks towards her, a storm in his eyes.

There's no dead boyfriend come back to life stalking her through the hospital. The blood is fake. The corridor is nothing but two walls in the middle of a studio stage. Camera operators move around her. Grips and gaffers and runners. None of them will meet her gaze.

Mo grabs her arm and drags her off the set and into the gloom behind a false wall. "Kitty, what the fuck is going on with you and this looking down at your shadow shit? That's nine takes now."

She pulls her arm free of his fingers and rubs at the white imprints they have left. "That hurt."

"Sorry," he says, holding up his hands. "Just frustrated. It's not that you're a woman – I'd handle a man in just the same way."

"Well, I guess that's okay, then," she says tartly.

"Come on, Kitty. Talk to me. I'm on a micro-budget, with Russian producers boasting little in the way of patience. Time's money and all that jazz. We're three days in and already they're getting twitchy." He strokes her arm, and she jerks it away. "I stuck my neck out for you. They wanted Abi Minto. But I said no, Abi's on the way down. Kitty is climbing towards the stars."

Mo is in his mid-forties, gym-trim and handsome in a too-pretty way, with a beard edged so neatly that Kitty concludes lasers must have been used. Not a look that floats Kitty Matthews' boat.

"What can we do to get beyond this?" he says.

"Edit out my shadow?" Kitty crosses her arms across her breasts in the hope it might encourage him to stop talking to them.

Mo gives a shake of his head followed by his *I'm sorry, did I hear that right?* expression. "What?"

"My shadow. It's ugly," says Kitty.

She sees fear and calculations in his eyes. She can almost hear him thinking: *Oh, my God! Am I too far in to replace her?*

She wants to explain herself. She wants to rant at him: *I spend my life eating the right food, not drinking what I want to drink, sleeping to the correct patterns, exercising until I want to weep and doing so much yoga I'm like a rubber fucking band, and the one thing I can't control is my shadow. And it's ugly. And it's going to fuck up my career if I don't do something about it. And most of all, my fucking shadow makes me remember... it makes me remember what happened. What used to happen. Remember him.*

But she just shouts, "Just digitally remove it or something."

Silence has fallen across the set. She senses that everybody is listening.

"Your shadow is ugly?" he repeats.

She nods.

"You want me to edit it out?"

Another nod.

"You'll get over it," he says and walks away, barking out for his assistant.

Blinking back tears, Kitty hurries towards her dressing room.

"Ms. Matthews?" It's a grip, moving to intercept her. He's Viking-huge with unruly facial hair and more ink than a Gutenberg press. In her opinion, he looks like ninety percent of grips.

"Fuck off," she says, holding out her palm towards him and glancing over her shoulder at her trailing shadow. She's not sure who she's swearing at.

Clear of the stage, she emerges into hazy sunlight, wiping away tears and cursing herself for being so weak. The air tastes of smoke. The wildfires that have savaged the country-side around the city have an insatiable appetite. The forests aren't enough for them. Now they're eating into the suburbs, consuming houses, cars, trash cans, cats, dogs, and people.

Kitty's phone beeps. She glances at the message on the screen. "Oh, for fuck's sake."

It's her mother.

"LADIES ARE we ready to order now?" says the smiling waiter, gliding to a stop beside their table. Late-evening sun angles into the restaurant and haloes him in scarlet. His shadow falls across the table. Kitty slides her phone from shade to light.

Her eyes devour the menu, calculating calories and the

capacity for dishes to bloat her stomach or dull her skin's lustre. Her options shrink to an unappetizing shortlist. Her stomach rumbles. Maybe she missed something. She studies the list again.

"Oh, do hurry up, Kitty," says her mother, Moira.

Kitty glances up catching her appraising the waiter with a cougar smile, shakes her head and returns to her interrogation of the menu.

"This darling man has other tables to serve, you know, and if you take any longer, the restaurant will be closed before we eat," says Moira.

"Give me a second," says Kitty.

"She's an actress," says Moira to the waiter. "Her body is a temple. Somewhere to chain up her soul and let it suffer for eternity. Something to let go dry and barren. Even Barnstable eats more than her." She indicates her dachshund sitting primly on the chair to her left, its diamante collar sparkling. She strokes the dog and coos.

Kitty imagines her mother strapped to the gurney in the hospital corridor. Imagines standing over her, scalpel in hand. Imagines her screaming and bleeding out under that flickering strip light.

"Healthy-heart omelette, with avocado carpaccio and pea shoot salad. No dressing." Kitty pokes the menu at the waiter, without looking at him.

Moira raises an eyebrow at the waiter. "Does that get your juices going?"

"It's one of our healthiest options," he replies.

"Hmmm…" says Moira, looking at his name badge. "Carlos, I'll have that lovely tuna steak you do so well here. Pink and moist, please. And I apologise for my daughter's rudeness."

When the waiter has left, Kitty leans forwards. "Do you have to belittle me in front of everybody?"

"Belittle?" Her mother makes a hacking noise at the back of her throat. "There was no belittling going on there. He couldn't take his eyes off you. He's probably seen one of your films. Which means he's seen quite a lot of you already. I mean, *really*, darling, do they write it into your contract that you have to dress like a cheerleader and show your breasts every fifteen minutes?"

Kitty smiles coldly. Moira continues to talk, telling her daughter that striving to look thin just makes you look fat. Telling her how she, Moira, the mother who never worked a day in her life, stays fit through force of will, and that this is enough to net her an endless string of younger lovers.

"When Gerald was alive, I was too busy tending to his needs to tend to my own, and..."

Gerald. Kitty's stepfather. *Tending to his needs. Tending to his needs? You know what that bastard's needs were. You know what he did to your daughters, to Mel and to me. You knew, and you did nothing. Now you paint a saintly portrait, hold it up to the sun and hide your failure in the shadows it throws.*

Kitty stops listening. The memory of her sister is too painful. She only hears sounds. A rattling buzz from her mother's maw. She imagines taking a surgical saw to Moira as she lies strapped to the gurney. Would she keep talking even after her head had been sawed off? Kitty wonders why she continues to give attention to this woman, this pretend mother, a woman who should have helped her, who should have a preternatural ability to sense her pain and to offer unconditional love and understanding, not to use her as a whetstone for her own narcissistic personality. Then, a word hooks her attention.

"What did you say?" says Kitty.

Her mother sips her Daiquiri, the salt making her curl her lips and bare her teeth. "I said, isn't it amazing how your shadow always looks fatter than your actual body?"

WHEN KITTY ARRIVES at the studio the next morning, sky heavy with ash and smoke, she's in such a funk that even though she *sees* the pretty redhead – hiding behind an ambulance, blowing a plume of cigarette smoke skywards, quickly ducking out of sight when she clocks Kitty – she doesn't devote enough brain space to actually *recognise* her.

Mo intercepts Kitty at the stage door and leads her to his office. Runs a finger along one edge of his precision-cut beard. His face is a mask of concern. Then he sacks her.

It's not working out, he tells her. Of course, he fought for her, fought like an alpha wolf protecting his mate, but the bean counters, being bean counters, can only see beans. And too many beans going in at the start means too few beans coming out at the end. The project is over schedule. The investors have spies on the set and they know who's causing the delays. They reminded Mo that they're funding Red Scalpel 3, not a Meryl Streep Oscar vehicle. Kitty is out, Abi Minto is in. Today. End of. It's re-shoot time.

Kitty remembers the ambulance. The young woman smoking. Hiding. Red hair. Abi Minto's *famously* red hair. She nods.

"Kitty?" Mo says. He's leaning forwards, a poor attempt at concern smeared across his face. His shadow slithers across his desk, onto her lap. "Do you understand what I'm saying?"

She feels numb.

"Kitty, you need to clear your dressing room."

She's out of the office. Striding across the set. The crew and cast watching and whispering. She's stuffing clothes into a bag. Books and makeup. Bag on her shoulder. She's leaving. Abi Minto approaches her, apologising, saying she's sorry, but Kitty waves her away, tells her she's welcome to it. That Mo is a cock, and the script is shit. And then there's a big man with a beard and tattoos and he's talking to her, but Kitty can't process his words. Shall I write it down for you? he says. Whatever, she says. He scribbles on a piece of paper and hands it to her. She stuffs it into a pocket and strides away, but then stops and turns around to face the big man.

"Want to go for a drink?"

"It's nine in the morning and I'm just about to start work," he says, holding out his hands, palms up. "Look, drinking may not—"

"Your loss," she says, and walks away.

───────

WHEN KITTY WAKES, she's lying in the recovery position. Her skull has been split into two pieces, filled with a writhing swarm of burning, winged needles, and then pressed back together into one ill-fitting whole. She opens her eyes. Sunlight punches her retinas.

The bar: amber shots lined up; laughter and music; a procession of faces.

Slowly, ever so slowly, she pushes herself upright. She's on her bed, fully clothed. She's alone. No depression on the opposite side of the bed. She sighs with relief, then dashes to the bathroom and, as the room tilts like a ship's deck in a storm, heaves up her guts. She strips off yesterday's clothes.

They smell subterranean. They smell of beer and bad memories. She imagines that's how her flesh must smell too. A piece of crumpled paper falls from the pocket of her jeans and she throws it into the bin.

She showers. Notices fingernail scrapes on the inside of one forearm. *Mo and his fake concern. The big grip pressing the note into my hand. Faces in the dark bar. An arm around my waist. Hot breath in my ear. Trying to pull myself free of clawing hands. Somebody wading in and throwing a punch, leading me up and out from the bar, under stars and neon and the burning sky and I'm collapsing, and it's the big grip again and my memories are all blurred and confused because he was there earlier in the day, not at the end.*

She needs coffee. No food. Her stomach wouldn't be able to stand food. She shuffles into her apartment's kitchen-living area and nearly jumps out of her skin when she sees the big grip asleep on the sofa. He's found a blanket from somewhere, but his torso, heavy with muscle, is uncovered. His skin is densely tattooed; an Illuminati eye at the centre of a pyramid, a pentangle, snakes and daggers, skulls and lines of text that might be Sanskrit.

"What the fuck are you doing in my apartment?" she shouts, flinching at the violence the sound inflicts on her fragile brain. She grabs a carving knife from the block on the kitchen counter.

"Whoa," he says, sitting up, blinking. "Calm down."

"I'm calling the cops." She shuffles towards the phone, keeping her eyes on him and the knife held out.

"Wait, I can explain." The grip offers open palms. "When you left the studio this morning, I could see you were in a bad way. And I know you've had a problem with drink in the past."

"So, you've been checking up on me, stalking me, you creep?"

"With respect, it's no big secret. I just read your Wikipedia entry when I got this gig."

She grabs the phone and dials 911 with her thumb, presses the phone to her ear.

A tiny voice escapes the phone's speaker. The grip talks quickly. "My day finished at three and I asked around to find out which bars you liked. When I found you, this scumbag was getting heavy with you. I taught him a lesson in manners and brought you home. I was going to go, but I didn't want you to choke on your own vomit."

Kitty stares at him. A small voice is her ear is asking about the nature of the emergency.

"Sorry, wrong number," she says, and hangs up. "What's your name?"

"Russ," he says. "Russ Havertz."

"Well, Russ Havertz, I'm not sure why you helped me, but thank you, I suppose. Although I'm sure I could have looked after myself, anyway. Now, please can you leave?" She's still holding the knife. She looks at it quizzically and slips it back into the knife block.

"Of course," says Russ, pulling on his long-sleeved T-shirt and lacing up his boots. "Did you call the number I gave you?"

"Number?" she says.

"The Shadow Lady." He stands and pulls on his jacket.

She remembers him walking alongside her as she left the studio; he was trying to explain something to her, but her head had been full of static. Only now does she remember this name: *the Shadow Lady*. The scrap of paper in the bathroom. She has no recollection of any context for the name.

"You don't remember, do you?" says Russ.

"Maybe not," she says, resenting this power he has over her. "How about you remind me?"

"Look, you may not be interested. It might be too far out for you. But I heard you talking to that dick, Mo. About wanting him to edit out your shadow. There are other ways. Older ways. If you really want it gone, speak to this woman."

"The Shadow Lady?" she says scornfully, even though she feels a thrill of excitement run through her.

"Yep, the Shadow Lady."

"Why?"

He hesitates before answering. "She can amputate your shadow."

Kitty can't stop the barking laugh escaping her. "Amputate? You're shitting me?"

"That's what I've been told," he says, shrugging.

"You ever see one of these amputated shadows?"

He shakes his head. "I was in a bad place before I sorted myself out. I mixed with some people who lived on the edge. I saw things. I didn't see *that*, but I saw enough to make me believe that if someone wanted to cut off a shadow, they could."

"Bullshit," she says.

"I saw a tattoo slide off a woman and strangle the dude she was sleeping with," he says, and his eyes are somewhere else.

Kitty points to the door. "I think you should leave now."

He goes. It's only then she remembers the scarring around Russ' throat.

HER AGENT CALLS. Her mother calls. Abi Minto calls. Incredibly, Mo calls, asking her out for a drink. She ignores them all. When the sun angles into her living room, she retreats to the bedroom and closes the shutters to avoid casting a hard shadow. She falls asleep and dreams about her stepfather. His shadow snaking into her bedroom, lying hot and heavy on her. Pressing down onto and into her.

She wakes with a start and tweaks a muscle in her neck. Pain radiates up the back of her skull and into her tongue. She goes to the bathroom, takes a painkiller, rescues Russ' crumpled slip of paper from the bin and returns to her bed. She stares at the number. Repeats it like a rosary.

Amputation. She shakes her head. "Bullshit."

Somehow the phone is in her hand. The dialling tone in her ear. She presses buttons. Two rings.

"Hello?" An unremarkable female voice, the hint of an accent. Softly spoken, possibly middle-aged.

"Is that... the Shadow Lady?"

"Some call me that, yes." She sounds amused, like a kind aunt who's just been called a cat lady. "I can be the Shadow Lady, if that's what you need. How can I help you, dear?"

How can I help you, dear? The question opens a yawning, cold chasm inside Kitty. But she doesn't know where to start.

"Can you make my shadow... go away?" she asks. She can't make herself say *amputate,* or *cut off,* or *kill.*

"What's your name?" says the Shadow Lady.

Kitty considers lying, but she's too tired for that. She tells her.

"Well, Kitty, I've helped people with similar requests. A penumbran may be a solution for you."

"A penumbran? What's that?"

"It's best if we meet to talk through the options. What you're seeking is complicated and there are risks involved; risks for you and for those around you. You have to be comfortable with them. And, without wanting to sound vulgar, there is the question of my fee, which is non-negotiable."

"Wait a minute," says Kitty. She hates the lack of control she has over this woman.

But the Shadow Lady doesn't wait. "I'm going to text you my fee, along with a neutral location. If the fee is acceptable, bring cash to that location tonight at eleven o'clock. My people will ensure you are not being followed; they will collect you and bring you to me. If the fee is too much, or if you change your mind, I'll understand. No hard feelings. But you must understand this is a one-time offer. The next time you call this number, the line will be dead."

Anger bubbles through Kitty. "Let me get this right. You want me to—"

A dialling tone buzzes in her ear. Kitty had been about to fire a barrage of scorn at the woman. This woman really thinks Kitty will just turn up God knows where, with a bag of cash? Does she think Kitty is an absolute idiot?

Her phone beeps. She reads the fee and the address. When she dials the number again, the line is dead.

KITTY WITHDRAWS the money from the bank. It's a sizeable amount, but she can easily afford it. One thing Mo had been truthful about was that, within the world of horror films, she is (or *was*) an actress on the rise. She'd made terrible films for very good money, then kept most of it so if the opportunity arose, she could afford to act in experimental films for peanuts.

She exits the bank, her shadow stretched long and ugly by the late afternoon sun. Her shadow fingers look like talons. She remembers Nosferatu's shadow creeping up the stairs in the film from the 1920s.

Does it know what I'm contemplating doing? Will it try to stop me?

She laughs at herself. It's obvious that she's going mad.

She doesn't go home. Time is running out for her to decide. She looks at the Shadow Lady's text message again. Checks the meeting point's location.

Instead of going there, Kitty drives to one of her favourite bars. It's underground. The lighting is low, no defined shadows, just a general gloom. She sits alone at a table and orders a bourbon. Just one for her nerves. But she has two. Russ texts her, asking if she's okay. How the hell did he get her number? She ignores him. Her mother calls, and Kitty ignores her too. A big man with a mane of swept-back hair and salt-and-pepper stubble saunters over and offers to buy her drinks. He reminds Kitty of her stepfather. She smiles at him, tells him to drop dead, and leaves.

An hour later, she's looking at her watch again: five minutes past eleven o'clock. She's downtown, standing on the junction of two nondescript side roads lit by hard streetlights. She can see the mountains surrounding the city, glowing red with wildfires. She can taste the forest's destruction at the back of her throat.

With her body wired and jumping at every noise, a shoulder bag containing a solid wad of notes clamped tight to her side, she may as well have a sign saying *Please come and mug me and live well for a couple of months* hanging around her neck. There's nobody waiting for her. And there's nobody coming. This is just some elaborate wind up, Russ and some of his friends having a laugh at her expense. They've probably got a camera rigged up somewhere, livestreaming her.

Then she sees the man on the opposite side of the road. He's tall and heavy-set, dressed in black jeans and a black bomber jacket that's struggling to contain an enormous belly. His face is covered by a smooth black mask, unmarked by any features other than two eyeholes. He stands motionless, obviously watching her.

"Shit." It comes out as a strangled whisper. Her car is parked a block away. She'd wanted to approach on foot so she could scope out the lie of the land. Why did she do that? Why didn't she just park up and wait in the car? Why does she always try to be clever? She knows she has to run – now. No time for hesitation.

"Kitty?" The soft female voice has Latino inflections and comes from behind her.

Kitty spins to face another black-clad, mask-wearing figure. She's a head shorter than Kitty with a generous figure.

"Are you Kitty?"

Kitty's breath comes rapidly. She glances down the shadowy street towards her car.

"We're not here to hurt you," says the woman, opening her arms and showing Kitty her palms. "It's up to you. You can leave now, or you can come with us to the Shadow Lady. In the interest of full disclosure, I need to say that if you come with us, we must blindfold you. But we'll be gentle. We're good at what we do."

Kitty looks back and forth between the two masked figures.

"So, are you in, or are you out?" says the woman.

This is ridiculous, Kitty thinks. *Madness. Nobody can make a shadow disappear.*

But despite these internal denials, she feels a thrill at standing on a precipice. The drop below her is enticingly unknown. At the very least, it offers the promise of distraction. To momentarily enjoy the exhilaration of falling, of escape, of the possibility of obliteration and the end of all this self-hate and doubt.

"In," says Kitty.

"Good." The woman waves an arm and a dark-blue van Kitty had thought was empty starts its engine, blinding her with its headlights. It pulls up alongside them and the side door swishes open.

"After you," says the masked woman, and Kitty climbs inside.

THE LATINO WOMAN is as good as her word. The blindfold plunges Kitty into darkness, but it sits comfortably around her head and over her eyes. When they arrive at their destination after a short drive, the man and woman carefully guide Kitty from the van and into an echoing space.

"Welcome to my studio," says a different woman, as Kitty's blindfold is removed. She recognises that slight accent, maybe German, from the phone call.

Kitty blinks as she stares around a large, empty warehouse which is mostly lost in darkness. The only illumination comes from dim lights above a couple of exit doors, and a standard lamp that sits alongside a desk with its surface covered by plastic containers. It's flanked by two chairs.

"Please, sit," says the woman, indicating the chairs.

"So, you're the Shadow Lady?"

The woman smiles. "Silly name, isn't it? Call me Lisbeth."

"Okay, Lisbeth it is," says Kitty.

They sit, and Lisbeth pops the lid from one of the plastic containers. She pushes it towards Kitty. "Blueberry muffin? I made them myself."

When Kitty imagined this meeting, the Shadow Lady had been a dark enchantress, alluring and frightening, probably deranged. She's nonplussed to be confronted by this maternal woman offering muffins. Lisbeth is probably in her mid-sixties, with grey hair pinned into an unruly pile, her skin wrinkled and pale, her lips glossy. She dresses trendily and expensively, like the owner of a high-end art gallery. The designer glasses perched on her nose completes the look. But her eyes are something else, bright blue and scalpel sharp. *That's where the true woman lives*, thinks Kitty. *In her eyes. I need to watch those eyes.*

"No thank you," says Kitty, waving away the muffins and patting her stomach. "I have to watch my figure."

"Well, it certainly is a figure worth watching. My, what I would have given for a figure like that when I was your age," says Lisbeth, those sharp eyes flicking over her. "Did you bring the money?"

Kitty is thrown by the sudden switch to commerce, but she unhooks the bag from her neck and places it on the table.

"Carlos," says Lisbeth, curling a finger, and the big man in the mask trots out of the shadows. "Be a darling and check it's all there, please."

When she says *darling*, it sounds like *darlink*. Without looking at Kitty, Carlos takes the bag and disappears into the shadows.

"It's not that I don't trust you. It's just good business practice," says Lisbeth, smiling again. "And I can use this time to explain my services and offer you one last opportunity to reverse your decision. If you do, that isn't a problem. Carlos will hand over your money and drive you back to where he picked you up. Once we start the process, there can be no return. Does that sound fair?"

Kitty nods, leans forward. In her mind, she's standing on that precipice again, excitement and fear rattling her every atom. "I need to understand what it is you actually do."

"Of course, of course," says Lisbeth, reaching out to pat Kitty's hand. "In the simplest of terms, I *part* you from your shadow."

"And you make the shadow disappear?"

"No, I cannot do that. What I do is to cut it away. Permanently. It doesn't disappear; it becomes an entity that is separate from you. We call this entity a penumbran."

"But what use it that? As soon as I go out in the sun, I'll have another shadow."

Lisbeth shakes her head. "You misunderstand. What I do is more profound. I take old magic and use it to break the natural laws. Once the penumbran is created, you will never cast a shadow again."

"That's impossible," says Kitty.

"Haven't you come to me asking for the impossible?" Lisbeth leans back in her chair and narrows her eyes. Her mouth is a tight line.

"Yes, but—" Kitty doesn't know what she wants to say.

"Child, I am not sure that this process is right for you. You're looking for help, but I clearly see you doubt you can receive it from me. You are looking for absence when all I can offer is separation. I feel this is a deal that we should not make."

"No, wait," says Kitty, sensing the precipice – and the release it offers – being moved away from her. She grabs Lisbeth's hand and instantly senses a large figure moving toward her through the shadows. It's Carlos, heading to his mistress' aid. Lisbeth waves him away.

"Please, Lisbeth," Kitty continues. "I want this. I do. It's just that, I... I can't... comprehend it."

Lisbeth pulls her hand from Kitty's grip and stares with her sharp eyes. "Okay, Kitty Matthews. It's rare I do this, but I see your pain. Carlos, a single light please."

Lisbeth's chair screeches against concrete as she rises. Kitty hears footsteps in the dark and then a bright light angles down into the centre of the warehouse from high above one of the exits. Kitty shields her eyes and looks up towards it, seeing two dozen or more enormous spotlights banked around it. The light reveals black symbols painted onto the floor.

Lisbeth walks out into the light and holds out her arms. Kitty feels the room move around her. She thrills at the impossibility of what she's seeing.

"You have no shadow," says Kitty, walking into the beam of light and seeing her own shadow stretch away behind her. "No shadow."

"No shadow, but a penumbran. Come here, my darling," says Lisbeth, calling into the darkness at the far side of the warehouse.

The shadow figure emerges from the gloom. Kitty takes a step backwards. She can see Lisbeth's features, younger but definitely hers, on the creature's shadow face. It stops alongside Lisbeth and squats low, legs wide, looking up at her adoringly like a loyal dog. Lisbeth reaches down and strokes its head. It pushes its shadow hair against her hand.

"Good girl," said Lisbeth, then shoos it away. "Wait in the other room. You know the big lights scare you." Reluctantly, the penumbran moves away from her, directing a reproachful glance at Kitty. At the edge of the room, it slips beneath a door as smoothly as a sheet of paper.

"But—" Kitty is lost for words. Fear and excitement trip each other in a tumble of thoughts.

Lisbeth ushers Kitty back to the table. "Penumbrans are fiercely loyal, and they hate to be separated from their source. It's important that you understand that what we create is dangerous. It is, in effect, a wild animal."

"But it's just shadow," says Kitty.

"No. A penumbran is not just a shadow. It can be what it chooses to be: insubstantial enough to slip beneath a door, or a solid thing that can break *through* a door. It is important that you understand this. We cut away a shadow, but we create a penumbran. A creature with agency. It will obey you, but it has a will. You have a responsibility to that creature."

"And bright lights scare it?"

Lisbeth nods. "Bright lights and daylight, most of all. They are creatures of the night. During the day they'll find a dark place to rest. They'll be nothing but a stain on the wall, a patch of deep shadow in a cupboard, or they may rest under floorboards. Some of my fellow practitioners think the penumbran is the root of the vampire myth."

Kitty has stopped listening to her. She is alive with the possibility of what she has seen. A shadow, twisted darkness made of terrible memories and fear, separated from her living body.

"I want this," she says, holding Lisbeth's gaze. "I *need* this."

Lisbeth scrutinizes her for what seems an age, then looks past her. "Is the money correct, Carlos?"

"Si, jefa," says Carlos, from the gloom.

"Then let us begin," says Lisbeth. "Take a seat. I need a few minutes to prepare."

Lisbeth sets Carlos to checking the intricate runes painted on the floor in a long oblong. She pops open a compact mirror and paints runes onto her cheeks and forehead as casually as if she was applying make-up for a downtown dinner date.

"Come." Lisbeth beckons Kitty and positions her on the only symbol painted in red. Kitty feels as if she is back on set again. The wall with the large bank of spotlights sits ten metres behind her. The rest of the warehouse stretches away into darkness.

"Take your position," says Lisbeth.

Carlos walks past them. His footsteps echo around the space. Kitty's heart races, chest rising and falling in deep heaves.

"Todo bien," says Carlos.

"Lights," says Lisbeth.

Even though she is facing away from the spotlights, so accustomed have her eyes become to the gloom that Kitty blinks against their intense glare. She feels their heat on her neck. Every inch of the warehouse is revealed by their brightness. It's empty, except for the long oblong of runes that stretches from her position to the far wall and, within their bounds, her shadow stretched long and wretchedly thin.

Lisbeth stands behind her, still casting no shadow even beneath these solar spotlights, and starts to chant. Kitty does not know what language she is speaking, but the rhythm of the words is hypnotic and repetitive. She becomes aware of her shadow in a way that she never has before. Not in a figurative way, representing as it does a part of her past she wants to obliterate, or her self-loathing, but in a physical way. As if she can actually feel it tugging against her body where she and it join, toe to toe. In the past she has attempted surfing a few times, the board tethered to her ankle to prevent it shooting away from her when she fell, and as the board moved in the surging tide, the tether would yank at her ankle, trying to pull her with it. This is the sensation she experiences now. Except it isn't just her ankle, it's her entire being.

Lisbeth's chanting increases in speed and volume. Words cascade over each other. She moves alongside Kitty and squats in a position that echoes that of her penumbran. She holds a small pot in one hand. She dips in a finger and draws a red line, bisecting Kitty's shadow, close to her feet.

Nausea floods Kitty's body. The shadow tugs wildly, unbalancing her. She feels unmoored, light-headed. Her arms go out at each side to steady her. There's nothing for her to hold on to.

Then the burning pain begins. It starts at her feet and rises through her body. She's a witch on a pyre, sweating and convulsing, but she can't move from the red painted symbol. The heat and pain come in sickening waves.

"What's happening to me?" She's not sure if the words leave her lips.

Lisbeth doesn't respond. Her chants are now shouted. Her red fingers are on the red line, digging in, tearing holes in the substance of Kitty's shadow as if it were latex. Kitty sees the long, dark shape, twist and writhe with movements wholly independent of her own. The pain is intense, overwhelming. She's going to faint. She's burning up. She needs to puke.

The shadow material is now ripping freely beneath Lisbeth's claws. Only slender tatters connect Kitty to her shadow. With a twist of a wrist, Lisbeth severs the remaining strand. An indescribable pain overwhelms Kitty, and she tumbles backwards, helpless as a marionette with snipped strings, watching her shadow – which moments before stretched a dozen metres – contract like a rubber band, snapping together into a perfectly proportioned shadow replica of Kitty. A sound like a gunshot echoes around the warehouse. Kitty lands on her backside and screams as the pain of separation consumes her. Her penumbran leans over her, screaming soundlessly in unison.

———

KITTY'S HANDS shake as she pours two-fingers' depth of brandy from bottle to glass. She slugs it back. She pours another measure. Her phone trills to signal an incoming message. She sets it to silent mode. Turns it over so she cannot see its flashing face. Turns it off. She never turns off her phone.

Moving into her apartment's sitting room, she places one arm beneath the light of a standard lamp. She feels heat on her flesh. Stares at the floor. Stares at the empty floor. She casts no shadow. But her arm feels heavy and painful. Her entire body throbs with a horrible ache, a pain that she cannot name.

The bottle and glass accompany her into the bedroom. She doesn't bother undressing, just clambers beneath the duvet, hugging herself. The burning heat of her separation from the penumbran has now been replaced by a bone-deep chill. She feels like she's coming down with flu. Her teeth chatter. Her entire body aches. Her stomach is filled with writhing eels. Within a minute, she's rushing to the bathroom and vomiting. She collapses onto the floor alongside the toilet and sobs.

It wasn't supposed to be like this. Separation from her shadow was supposed to be a joyful liberation, a shedding of memories and dead skin, not this soul-deep feeling that she's betrayed herself. That she's actually finished the work that her stepfather started; mutilating herself beyond repair.

She remembers the moments following separation. The enormous spotlights were extinguished, Lisbeth helping her to her feet, telling her that *Yes, separation is always this painful, everybody feels the nausea, this ache. It will pass, with time.*

Everybody recites this sort of cant when they're ill or injured. Everybody promises an end to the horror, but it's a lie. It's always a lie.

As Kitty had stood, her penumbran had squatted in a subservient pose, just as Lisbeth's had done earlier. The sense of shock and wonder at the thing before her was momentarily enough to distract Kitty from the pain. The penumbran was a perfect copy of her in shadow. Every individual strand of shadow hair moving naturally, shadow sclera, shadow irises and shadow pupils, shadow pores on shadow skin, shadow chest rising and falling, shadow shirt and shadow jeans.

Kitty had reached out and stroked the penumbran's head, tangling her fingers in its hair, marvelling at the impossibility of its solidity. It pushed against her palm like a dog luxuriating in its mistress' attention, eyes peering up to meet hers, something fundamental and needy in its gaze. There was love in those eyes, and it terrified Kitty.

"Go!" She had yanked her hand back as if from flames. Took a step back from the penumbran.

"What are you doing?" asked Lisbeth.

"Go on, run. Get away from me now!" Kitty had shouted the words, stamping her foot close to the penumbran. Still squatting, it had shuffled away from her, cowering, a dog expecting a beating but still hoping for forgiveness. "Get away from me. I never want to see you again!" she screamed.

Lisbeth had grabbed her arm, shouting words at her: *dangerous... separation... wild animal... murder...* but Kitty had just pulled her arm free and screamed at the penumbran, raising a hand. She'd advanced upon it, watching it finally scuttle away from her, throwing one last pleading look at her before it bared its teeth like a baboon and hurried away on all fours into the gloom at the far end of the room. The banging of a door echoed around the warehouse.

"Why?" said Lisbeth. "After everything I told you. After all that pain; why?"

"I'm clean now," said Kitty.

But Kitty feels far from clean. She feels soiled, guilty and dead inside. Pain racks her body, shuddering aches where her shadow should be. Phantom pains for a phantom limb. She's too tired to lever herself off the bathroom floor. She falls asleep beside the toilet.

———

TIME LOSES MEANING. It's elastic. Redundant. Why measure time when you feel the same devastating ache every second of your existence, whether you are awake, asleep or a mix of the two? At some point, Kitty crawls from the bathroom into the bedroom. The faintest hint of red light where she hasn't properly secured her blackout curtains. There's a tang of smoke in the air. Maybe she's in hell. She clambers into bed. It's like hiking a mountain. She sleeps again.

Hiking. Climbing.

Kitty is in a car with her stepfather, Gerald, her mother and older sister Mel. School's out and they're going hiking in the mountains. Her stepfather is driving. The stink of his cologne is choking her. He's angry and uncommunicative. It's not an unusual state for him. Mother stares out of the window. Mel does the same. The silence is mud thick and makes it hard to breathe. What's happened? Why is everybody being like this? Kitty doesn't understand. She tries to make conversation, but all she can elicit are monosyllabic answers. She makes a joke, but nobody laughs. Gerald turns up the radio: classical music; it's all he listens to. Boring, says Kitty, and he snarls at her. She's quiet after that.

They park and start to walk. Without a word to the rest of the family, Gerald strides off on his own, climbing a path up the mountain. He has a heavy limp, a consequence of a skiing accident that left him with a metal bar holding together his shattered right femur. Mother calls him back, but Gerald ignores her. When Mel sets off in pursuit of Gerald, Kitty is left looking back and forth between her scattering family. She doesn't understand what's happening, so runs after her big sister, leaving her mother behind.

Mel is sixteen, six years older than Kitty. Mother had miscarriages between them. The big age difference has never been a problem. They have always been fast friends, and Mel is everything that Kitty wants to be. She watched her older sister change from a gangly, spotty youth to a confident, intelligent young woman who made saucer-eyed skater boys spill from their boards as she confidently strode by, quoting Shakespeare and Kerouac in her cut-off denims and a crop top.

And then something happened. Almost overnight. Kitty was forced to watch that beautiful blossoming reverse. She watched her sister becoming uncommunicative, moody, easily upset. Watched her confidence evaporate and be replaced by anger and anxiety.

"Mel, wait for me," she says.

But Mel ignores her, speeds up, those long legs scissoring purposefully. Kitty has to run to catch up.

"What's up?"

"Go back, little sis."

"Why?"

"Just do it, okay."

"No, I won't."

Mel spins, and squatting down grabs Kitty's little arms. Her grip is so tight it hurts Kitty. But what hurts more is the sight of Mel crying. That's painful *and* scary. "I love you, Piglet. You're my best friend, okay? But today you have to do what I say," says Mel.

Kitty shakes her head.

"Listen to me, Kitty." Mel's eyes are imploring her. "Go back to Mum, please."

Another shake of her head. "I'm coming with you."

"You can't."

"Why?"

"Because I say, okay? This is important. I have something to do."

"But we're climbing the mountain." Kitty wants the day to be as simple as she had imagined it. The family goes out together. The family climbs the mountain. The family have their picnic, laugh and joke, and then the family goes home and lives happily ever after.

Mel scrubs away tears. The tone of her voice changes. She points back down the track to where their mother has come into view, plodding slowly up the incline. "Go back to Mum. I don't want you with me."

She stands and turns. Kitty grabs her hand, but Mel snatches her hand free. "Leave. Me. Alone." She pushes her little sister in the chest and Kitty stumbles backwards, landing heavily. Mel moves to help her, then checks herself. "Don't follow me." She runs up the track after Gerald.

Everything after that is a blur of images. Images that bleed together. Climbing the track with her mother, who is repeating something over and over under her breath. The sun splitting into iridescent beams as it breaches the cover of fir trees. A lost seagull calling. The sound of Mel and Gerald arguing up ahead. Kitty's breath rushing in and out as she tries to keep up with her mother's half-walk, half-run. The seagull swooping low again, screaming. Another scream; Mel's scream. Her mother sprinting, leaving Kitty. The rising path seen through tears. Mother confronting Gerald. *What have you done?*

"She jumped," says Gerald. "I tried to stop her. She was depressed. You know that."

Kitty looks over the cliff edge. Far below, on a rock outcrop coloured ochre by the sun, lies Mel.

There is somebody behind Kitty. Fingers stroke her hair.

FINGERS STROKE HER HAIR. Kitty wakes. She expects to see blue sky, bright sun, her sister's long limbs at awkward angles, but she's in the pitch black of her bedroom. Somebody stroked her hair. Not in the dream, in the here and now. She's frozen, listening. The room is silent. She wills her eyes to adjust to the darkness. She senses movement. A patch of more profound darkness circling the bed. She can smell smoke, as if somebody has brought the stench of the wildfire into her apartment.

Frantically, she fumbles to turn on the bedside light, blinking as it blinds her. She scoots backwards so she's pressed against the headboard, legs tight to her chest. Wardrobe, clothes rail, standing mirror, the high-backed green velvet chair she bought at the weekend market (the man told her Elvis had owned it, but she didn't believe him), a belt snaking across the floor, discarded yoga clothes in the corner, a pink gym ball and matching dumbbells – her bedroom. No intruder. Nobody to stroke her hair. It was the dream. That bloody dream!

Her mouth is as dry as burnt timber. The glass on her bedside table is empty. As she swings her legs free of the duvet, a shadow hand shoots out from under her bed and grabs her ankle. She screams and, wrenching herself free, tumbles forward, landing on knees and elbows. The penumbran is beneath her bed. It slithers free, expanding, reaching for her, eyes pleading.

Kitty locks herself in her bathroom. The fluorescent light is reassuringly bright. It buzzes gently.

"Leave me alone!" she screams. "Go away."

She stares down at the gap at the bottom of the bathroom door, remembering Lisbeth's words. *It can be what it chooses to be; insubstantial enough to slip beneath a door, or a solid thing that can break through a door.*

She presses her ear against the wood. There is no sound from the bedroom. But she knows that it's there, on the other side of this thin wooden barrier. She'd known it was the penumbran from the moment she woke because the overpowering ache of separation had vanished. Mixing with the horror of home invasion, of the sudden shock of that hand reaching out from beneath the bed to grab her ankle, was the seductive sensation of reunion, of relief, of pleasure.

"Please leave me alone!" she shouts again.

Her neighbours in the apartment below thump on their ceiling. She can hear the outline of their curses.

Kitty sits on the toilet looking at the door, but the penumbran doesn't enter. The throbbing, dull ache returns to her body slowly. The penumbran is leaving her. Moving away into the near-dawn shadows.

She takes almost an hour to pluck up the courage to re-enter her bedroom, whipping aside the blackout curtains to reveal the orange skyline – sunrise and wildfire. She searches her entire apartment. She's alone. Hands shaking, she makes coffee. She's not sure she'll ever be able to sleep again. Her body is in revolt. Every muscle on fire. Tears spread concentric rings across her coffee.

"What have I done?" she says, and nobody answers. "Come back. Please come back."

Her phone beeps. It's her mother.

"JESUS, Kitty, you really look awful today," says Moira.

"Thanks, Mom. You look lovely too."

Kitty has met her mother in a neighbourhood coffee shop – *Make Joe Slo* –close to Kitty's apartment. Moira had wanted to meet her for breakfast at a new *destination restaurant* with the *most* amazing breakfasts, across town. Kitty refused. It had taken all her energy to drag herself here, and she was even now cursing her weakness, her inability to refuse this narcissist's requests. She hasn't touched the coffee or bagel and cream cheese before her. The smoky light outside colours her knife red. The wildfires are getting closer.

"I think I'm coming down with a bug, that's all," she says, taking mild satisfaction as her mother shifts minutely away from her.

"You should have told me. I don't want to get ill, not when my psychic and emotional defences are low," says Moira. She pushes her floral scarf up under her nose. "Francis is being beastly to me. I think it might all be over."

Francis is her mother's latest toy-boy lover. She'd snared him when he was cleaning her pool, or servicing her car, or fixing the air-conditioning – something like that. Domestic maintenance situations are Moira's favourite hunting ground.

The dachshund, Barnstaple, sitting on a cushion next to his mistress, stares at Kitty and growls. His top lip ripples like a caterpillar in motion, revealing pearly white teeth. Normally he's aloof, refusing to acknowledge Kitty's presence. Today, he's reacting to her as if she's a threat.

"Oh, baby. Barnstaple's very sensitive to illness, aren't you, my little prince?" Moira bends to kiss the top of his chestnut head. "He can tell there's something off with you today."

"I told you, it's just a bug."

"No," says Moira, squinting at her. "There's something else. I can't put my finger on it."

Barnstaple yaps at Kitty and Moira bends low, hushing him. The dachshund ducks away from her ministrations, keeps his doggy gaze fixed on Kitty. His little body trembles as he takes a breath and redoubles his growling.

Only now does Kitty realise just how much she hates this dog. A dog that has had more love and attention, more indulgences lavished on him, than either of Moira's daughters. *Look at it, sitting on its purple cushion that she transports everywhere, diamante collar glittering, that imperious tilt of its head.* She looks down at her red-tinted knife and wonders if it'd be sharp enough to do the mutt damage. Instead, with her mother's attentions still focused on the dog, Kitty bares her teeth at him and releases an almost inaudible hiss.

It's too much for the dog. He slips free of Moira's hands and wedges himself between her back and the plush banquette.

"Oh, Barnstaple, what's the matter, darling?" Moira twists and scoops him into her arms.

Kitty has had enough. She can't deal with this today. It's a battle for her to be civil to her mother in normal circumstances, but now, with the ache of loss wracking her body and clouding her mind, she just cannot deal with her.

"What did you do to him?" says Moira. "Why is everybody being beastly to me at the moment?"

Kitty opens her mouth, but her mother presses on.

"You're my daughter. You're supposed to be there for me in my later years. That's the deal. I look after you when you're young, you look after me when I'm old. Well, I'm not old, but you understand what I mean."

Suddenly, the knife is in Kitty's hand. Red blade. Red light. The ache throbbing through her body. She can't think clearly. She needs her mother to shut the fuck up. Then she's plunging the knife into her mother's right eye socket. Pulling her hand away. The ruins of Moira's eye is running down her cheek. Barnstaple is howling. Moira is screaming.

"Are you listening to a word I'm saying?" says Moira.

Kitty slips out of the violent daydream, focuses on the now. It takes a supreme effort of will. She hasn't murdered her mother. She doesn't know if she's relieved or disappointed.

"I'm going," says Kitty, standing suddenly, her chair screeching against the flooring. People turn and stare. Kitty is swaying on the spot.

"What?" Moira looks horrified. "We haven't discussed what I'm going to do about Francis."

"I don't care," she says. "I'm not well today."

And then she's out of *Make Joe Slo* and on the street. And the sky is red and stinks of smoke. And her body is burning up and broken and incomplete. And she knows where to find the bars that open at this time in the morning.

———

SHE'S in another subterranean bar, the sort with lighting so low it doesn't throw shadows. Her body aches unbearably. She tries to focus on her hatred of Barnstaple, of her mother. She doesn't want to remember, but she can feel the memory clambering up from the dark pit, the depths of her mind. Three drinks in, the memory breaches her defences.

Mel is dead. Her funeral was a week ago. The young Kitty is numb and confused. She feels incomplete. Like somebody has snapped off a piece of her body. She doesn't know how to function, doesn't know where the edges of things are anymore.

Her mother and stepfather are alien beings; their shouted arguments senseless, the way they act towards each other bizarre. Mostly, her mother is a ghost, drifting around the house, her mind clouded by sedatives. She cries frequently, rises late and stays up into the early hours staring at the television. The volume is too loud, you can hear it throughout the house. It's like she's trying to drown out any lingering echoes of Mel. She barely talks to Kitty and tries to ignore Gerald. She and Gerald are sleeping in different bedrooms. Kitty doesn't know what this means, but it scares her. She tries to reach her mother, curling up next to her on the sofa, pressing her body against her, but there is no acknowledgement. Kitty thinks her mother has retreated deep inside, to a cave at the centre of this lump of flesh. Her mother feels nothing on the surface anymore, barely knows that the outside world is there.

Gerald has changed too. Before Mel's death, he had no time for Kitty. Mel was his special girl – that's what he called her – and he trailed her like a shadow. Suddenly, he is overly solicitous with Kitty. He guides her away from her mother, whispering that her mom needs time and space and a place to grieve. I'll look after you, he says, and his arms snakes around her shoulder and strokes her back. The smell of his cologne is disgusting. He plants a kiss on her cheek. Her skin crawls, but she doesn't know why.

And then the shadow comes.

It's midnight. Moira must be up still because Kitty can hear the laugh track of a sitcom. Her bedroom door opens, and the shadow slides into the room, slowly crossing the floor, climbs onto the bed and lays heavy on her. She gags on the smell of cologne.

I'll look after you, says the shadow.

The shadow will return, at least once a week, for the next two months, until Gerald suddenly dies of a heart attack. Welcome as his death is, it's too late for Kitty; her own shadow has already been corrupted and bent into something ugly, something irredeemable, by his nighttime visits.

A stubbled barfly makes his way towards Kitty but turns to head back to his own table when he sees her face streaked by tears, a bubble of snot inflating below one nostril.

"Well, it's gone now," says Kitty, raising her glass and draining it of amber fluid. "Bye bye shadow."

She scrubs away snot and tears with a sleeve and pushes back her chair. Normally, once she starts drinking, she doesn't stop until she finds oblivion. Today, fatigue and the rabid ache consuming her body overpowers this urge. One more drink will have her spewing over the table.

She pays the barman and heads back to her apartment, closes the curtains on the burning skyline, strips and collapses into bed. Blessed sleep pulls her deep.

THERE'S somebody in the room. Kitty is sure of this as soon as she jerks awake, heart lurching like an animal trapped in a bag. The room is in total darkness, but she can sense and smell a presence; smoke accompanied by the stink of raw meat. Something else has changed, something inside her she cannot identify while her internal alarms are screaming *intrusion*.

"Who's there?" She pats her bedside table, feeling for the lamp. She can't find it. Where the hell is it? She hears a sound.

Tap. Tap. Tap.

God, please, please, let me find the switch. Instead, her fingers find the glassy lozenge of her phone and she swipes and taps, cursing, breath coming in pants, as she tries to turn on its torch app.

That's not tapping, that's dripping, she thinks.

Drip. Drip. Drip.

The phone's torch blazes into life and, blinking at its brilliance, she shines the beam at the bottom of her bed. What she sees makes her scream and push herself back against the wall. She drops the phone, reducing its light to an orange halo around its body.

"Leave me alone!" she shouts.

In the momentary glare of the light, she'd seen her lamp lying on its side, on the floor beyond her bedside table. She must have knocked it over when she slumped into bed. She lurches through darkness, grabs the lamp and turns it on. The room fills with light.

The penumbran squats at the foot of her bed, a glossy brown and bloody shape dangling from its mouth. It's Barnstaple. The dachshund's eyes are lifeless and a coil of grey intestine dangles from its belly. Blood drips from his torn stomach.

Drip. Drip. Drip.

The penumbran drops Barnstaple and looks at Kitty with pleading eyes. Looks at her with her own eyes. *Oh Christ, it's brought me the dog as a gift, a tribute*, she thinks. Kitty remembers her encounter with Moira and Barnstaple earlier that day. She'd fantasised about killing the dog with a butter knife. Was she the cause of this? Had the penumbran read her thoughts and acted on them? She'd also fantasied about stabbing her mother in the eye. Had she met a similar fate?

As if answering the question, her phone rings. The name Moira flashes on the screen. Kitty doesn't answer. The phone stops ringing and a message pops up, informing her she has voicemail. A few seconds later a SMS message appears: *Barnstaple missing! I don't know what to do! Call me!!!!!!!*

Kitty releases a deep sigh, letting the tension out of her body, and simultaneously realises what else has changed. The bone-deep ache of separation has gone. The proximity of the penumbran, her shadow, the missing part of herself, has brought relief to that agony. In fact, it has gone beyond relief to pleasure. A narcotic glow is settling on her, the sort of cloudy relief brought on by strong opiate pain medication.

The penumbran nudges the dog's corpse towards Kitty and creeps closer to the bed. It presses against the mattress. The bed shakes. It yearns for her to accept the gift.

Kitty closes her eyes and takes several deep breaths. Even this small increase in proximity amplifies the pleasant sensations washing through her. After a day of ugly pain, she savours the feelings. Her extremities are tingling.

Her initial alarm and horror are melting away under this wave of pleasure, and she thinks: *Maybe I was wrong. This shadow isn't him. It's me. It's the me he damaged. The damaged me. I shouldn't fear it. I should pity it. I should try to help it. Maybe I can even heal it, and perhaps that will heal the whole me? Does it matter that a dog has died to earn me a small revenge? It's not as if it has hurt a person. Compared to what happened to me, it's nothing.*

She releases an enormous yawn. The pleasant sensations, the waves of relief, are falling on her like warm duvets, one after another.

She picks up her phone and, with increasingly uncoordinated fingers, replies to her mother's message: *Oh dear. I'm sure you'll find him.* Then she turns the phone to silent and lays it face down on the bedside table.

Kitty faces the penumbran, yawning again. "You can stay for tonight. We'll see how things look tomorrow. Okay?"

Joy fills the shadow's face as it nods and clambers up onto the bed on all fours.

"Wait—" says Kitty, then relents. "Okay, but stay on the end of the bed."

The penumbran, turning in a slow circle, wraps itself into a cat-like coil pressing against her feet through the duvet. Another wave of relief washes through Kitty at the penumbran's touch. She can't keep her eyes open. She's high as a kite, floating on clouds; all she can think are pleasant cliches.

She sleeps and doesn't dream.

Or does she dream?

She is lying on her side with somebody behind her. Fingers run through her hair as if they were a comb's teeth. Lifting strands and letting them fall gently onto her neck. The touch is light and expert. It's something she would do to herself in idle moments on set; eyes distant, savouring the sensation.

The fingers drift down to her neck and shoulders. The touch is featherlight, just as she likes it. She shivers with pleasure, keeps her eyes closed. There's a naked body pressing against her back, moulding itself to the curve of her flesh. It's a female body. She realises what is happening, even though she isn't sure if it is real or imagined. It's *my* body, she thinks; *my shadow body, my penumbran. It's so close to me that all the pain has gone and been replaced by pleasure. So much pleasure.*

The shadow holds her tight, arms around her, a leg crooked over her body. She is in a cage of shadow limbs when she sleeps again.

WHEN KITTY WAKES the next morning, she is alone in the bed. No cage of limbs. No penumbran curled at her feet. Had she actually allowed it to hold her like that? Or had that been a dream?

She senses her penumbran is nearby. The aching pain of separation hasn't returned, but the narcotic euphoria of reunion has dissipated and been replaced by a sensation that she is being watched. That covetous eyes are crawling over her.

Why did I let it hold me? There had been the voice in her head telling her it was okay, but had those been her own thoughts or the penumbran's?

She rises and rushes to pull on an oversized T-shirt and leggings, feeling a desperate need to cover her nakedness. In her haste, she nearly steps onto a dark shape on the floor, remembering Barnstaple's corpse just in time. She opens the curtains, letting in a blaze of red-tinged light. She glimpses movement in the corner of the room, a shadowy silhouette hastily squeezing itself into the darkness beneath her bed.

Barnstaple's corpse draws her gaze. Its little body is rigid, eyes lifeless, a coil of intestines forming a question mark amidst the bloody mess released from its bitten belly.

In the kitchen, her hands shake as she pulls on rubber gloves and grabs a refuse sack. Taking a deep breath, she steadies herself against the work surface. She doesn't want to return to the bedroom, to the penumbran. She wants to flee her apartment and never return. She checks her thoughts. Hadn't she wished Barnstaple dead, only for the penumbran to make it happen? It'd been inside her head. What would it do to *her* if she let it know how fearful of it she really was? That she wanted to flee?

She calms her mind with a yoga technique, focusing on her breathing, and returns to the bedroom. As she kneels beside Barnstaple, she glimpses the penumbran watching her from beneath her bed, a glimmer of red light reflected on a black pupil.

Keep breathing, keep counting.

Turning her head away and wincing with disgust, she lifts Barnstaple's rigid body and drops him into the black bag, knotting the top. The body has left a bloody stain on the carpet. She returns with a bucket of water and cloth and scrubs it clean. Pink water circles in the sink as she pours it away.

She picks up the phone and dials her local pizza house. It's closed. She gets a recorded message.

"Hi Jenny, you still on for this morning?" she says. "Cool, see you at the class. Looking forward to it too."

Kitty hangs up, returns to the bedroom and changes into her yoga gear. Tops it off with a hoodie and baseball cap. Grabs her sunglasses, car keys, apartment keys.

Keep breathing, keep counting.

She thinks she sees movement out the corner of her eye, but she doesn't stop, moving purposefully from bedroom to living room and to the front door. She unlocks the door. Breathing, counting, waiting for a hand to close around her face and drag her back into the apartment.

She locks the door behind her. She runs down the stairs; there's no time to wait for the elevator. The underground car lot is dark and echoing, and she wants to fill it with screams. She fumbles open her car door and jabs the key into the ignition even as she pulls the door closed.

Then she sees the shadow in the back seat, and screams. But it's only a dress she was going to wear to a friend's party, still in its dry-cleaning bag, hanging from a hook. She's laughing and crying as she drives up the exit ramp and into bright sunlight.

Kitty drives to a local recreation field where smiling families watch their kids flinging baseballs back and forth. She finds a place to park away from all their pretty picnics and laughter. Then she wraps her arms around herself and lets the screams and tears come.

"RUSS, GET OVER HERE." Kitty is peering out from behind the wreckage of a spaceship, waving an arm at the grip.

"Kitty?" he says, looking confused.

"Don't broadcast it."

Frowning and glancing around to make sure he isn't being watched, Russ hurries over to her. "What the hell are you doing here?"

"Looking for you," says Kitty.

Russ glances over his shoulder. They're outside one of the major sets, amidst a clutter of props for an upcoming science-fiction film. Technicians and extras move purposefully between buildings.

"If Mo sees me talking to you, it'll be adios, Russ. He's got it in for you," says Russ.

"Like I give a shit," says Kitty. "And that's nothing compared to what I'll do to you if you don't help me."

"Whoa, lady—"

Kitty cuts him off. Jabs a finger in his chest. "I need to speak to the Shadow Lady, like, yesterday."

"The Shadow Lady?" Russ looks at the ground behind her and raises his eyebrows. "So, you did it. I thought there was something different about you."

"Yes, I did it, and now I'm well and truly fucked, no thanks to you."

"Now wait just a minute, I didn't make you do anything. I gave you a number and a name, that's it. Whatever happened afterwards was your choice."

"Yes, but... I wouldn't... I wouldn't have even known about her if it wasn't for you."

Kitty is shaking. The pain of separation feels like nails hammered into her bones. She's feverish again. The weirdness of the previous night, her lack of control, what she'd allowed to happen, the dead dog, the eyes watching her from beneath the bed – it's all too much. She presses her face into her hands and releases a sob.

"Hey steady," says Russ, stepping forwards and wrapping his arms around her.

"Don't touch me!" Kitty pushes him away. "I need a number for her. Today. Okay? Please, I'm begging you to help me. Something bad is going to happen if I don't fix this quickly. If it helps, her actual name is Lisbeth. Just talk to one of your killer tattooed friends or something."

"Kitty, I—"

"Please, Russ." There are tears on her cheeks. She's shuffling on the spot like a junkie trying to score crack. She lowers herself to one knee. "You want me to get down on my knees?"

He pulls her up. "Stop it. What's happened?"

"I don't want to talk about it, okay? I *can't* talk about it. I just need you to do what I asked. Please."

Russ sighs, twisting to look anxiously over each shoulder in turn. "Lisbeth, you said her real name was?"

Kitty nods. "Uh-huh."

"Okay, look, I'll try, but—"

"Thank you," she says, nodding, blinking away tears.

"I can't promise anything."

"Call me," she says, turning.

"Kitty—"

But she's hurrying away, using her sleeves to scrub her

cheeks clear of tears, ramming on her sunglasses, head down beneath the sunlight, casting no shadow.

SHE SITS in a park and composes herself, counting her breaths, trying to think away the pain. Kids squeal as they run through a fountain. Music thumps nearby. Tennis balls *thwack* back and forth. Joggers pass her, trailing shadows. The trees above her cast spider-web shadows. Shadows everywhere. The entire world has a shadow. How could she have thought that losing hers would change her life?

"Fucking idiot!" she barks out, laughing bitterly. A young mother in pastel workout gear, ponytail bobbing jauntily, hurries past her, pushing a pram.

Kitty moves to a cafe, but she can't taste the coffee. She visits a gallery, but she sees no art, just a blur of colour. Somebody approaches her and asks for an opinion on a cubist landscape. Kitty ignores her. All she can concentrate on is controlling the pain. She wanders the streets, counting and breathing, breathing and counting, and people curve their trajectories to give her a wide berth.

By early evening, as dusk falls, she's exhausted by fighting the pain. Russ hasn't called. She can't take this anymore. Despite her fear of the penumbran, her fear of herself, she drives back to her apartment. Every street closer to home lessens the pain and releases the unsettling feeling of euphoria. She cannot win. Pain and joy are both equally threatening. By the time she pulls into her space in the underground car lot, the pain has almost disappeared.

Her car beeps as she locks the door. Footsteps echo in the gloomy space and she quickens her pace, looking behind her, willing her eyes to penetrate the darkness. But the shadow isn't behind her. It emerges from behind a pillar directly in front of her and instinctively she lashes out.

"OW!"

Kitty took self-defence classes a few years ago, and those learned reflexes kick in. She lands a satisfyingly, solid punch on the side of her attacker's nose, then lunges forwards with her knee, ready to strike him in the groin, halting the strike at the last second when she recognises the man.

"Mo?"

"Jesus, Kitty. Why did you do that?" he says, clutching a hand to his face. Blood drips between his fingers. "I think you broke my nose."

"You scared the crap out of me, you dick. What the hell are you doing here?"

"I'm bleeding," he says, pinching his nose and tipping his head back. "Do you have any tissues, a handkerchief, something?"

"You're lucky you're not wearing your balls for earrings," says Kitty, adrenalin still singing in her ears as she roots around in her handbag. "I don't have anything."

"Can I come up and get something to stop the bleeding?" asks Mo.

Kitty crosses her arms. "No, you can't. What do you want, Mo?"

"Please. I can't talk like this. Let's just say I have good news for you." He smiles. There's blood running over his cheek, blood on his teeth.

A car pulls into the far end of the car lot. She doesn't want her neighbours seeing her talking to a bloody-faced film director, who's just sacked her from a high-profile project, in an underground car lot. The last thing she needs is the police knocking on her door.

"You can clean up, then go, deal?" she says.

"Whatever you say," says Mo.

With his head tipped back horizontally, Kitty leads Mo into the elevator and up to her floor. She thanks providence that there's nobody entering or exiting the neighbouring apartments. As she flicks on a light, heart lurching as the darkness retreats, she half expects the penumbran to come bounding up to her like a dog welcoming home its mistress. Nothing happens. No movement. No sound other than a refrigerator hum. But she knows the penumbran is in the apartment. She can feel the waves of relief unleashed by its proximity.

"We going in, or what?" Mo sound like he's gargling blood.

She shows Mo to the bathroom and leaves him to clean himself up. When she hears water running, she crosses to her bedroom and pushes open the door.

Calm thoughts, only calm thoughts. Show it no fear. Don't think about Russ. Don't think about Lisbeth.

The penumbran is squatting at the foot of her bed. A smile splits its face, and it lurches across the room on all fours like a baboon, pushing its head into her lap, hands stroking the backs of her legs, then rising and embracing her. She's almost overwhelmed by a head rush as strong as any narcotic she's tried, which is most of them. She wants to give in. To press herself even closer, to be whole again, but she pushes it away.

Confusion creases its face. It reaches for her again.

"No, stay in here, okay? There's a man here. He can't see you."

The penumbran strokes her face.

"Stop." She allows anger to enter her voice as she grabs its wrists and holds them away from her. The penumbran's face ripples with a wholly unhuman expression.

"He's a dangerous man – we can't let him see you. Do you understand?" She's smiling, pleading.

The penumbran nods. It's a very slow, unnatural movement. Kitty can hear Mo finishing up in the bathroom.

"Good. I'll be with you soon," she says, slipping out of the room and closing the door.

She takes deep breaths, straightens her clothes and enters the living room just as Mo emerges from the bathroom. His nose has stopped bleeding, but it looks red and there are spots of blood down his otherwise pristine white shirt.

"Who were you talking to?" he asks.

"My mother. On the phone," Kitty says. She waves an arm towards the front door. "Time to go."

Mo unleashes his brilliant smile, an effective advert for his orthodontist and now clean of blood. "Aren't you interested in hearing my good news?"

"I'm not interested in hearing anything from you. If you've forgotten, you humiliated me by sacking me from a film that was going to make my career, just a couple of days ago. Time to go – come on." She sweeps an arm towards the door again.

Mo ignores the gesture and his gaze sweeps over the apartment. "Nice place."

"Mo, you need to go."

Instead of leaving, Mo lowers himself onto the sofa and man-spreads to ninety degrees. "Why were you at the studio today? I saw *you*, talking to one of my grips. It all looked a bit... heated. He your boyfriend?"

"None of your goddamn business."

Mo gives her his smile again and his gaze slides over her body, from her face to her feet, as if he's choosing from a menu. "Or were you hoping to bump into me?"

Kitty slips her phone from her pocket. "I'm calling the police unless you leave."

"I don't think so," says Mo, laughing lightly and leaning further back into the sofa. His man-spread widens. He pats the sofa cushion next to him. "Sit here and I'll tell you something that I guarantee will change your mood from suspicion and anger to delight and gratitude."

Her finger hovers over the phone's screen. She needs him out of her apartment, but she needs the police here even less. Not with the penumbran squatting in her bedroom. She knows she can't physically eject Mo; she isn't strong enough. *How am I going to get this lizard out of my apartment?* With a sickening feeling, she realises her only option is to indulge him and hope that he just goes away.

With a sigh, she slips the phone back into her pocket – noticing his smile widen – and lowers herself onto the opposite end of the sofa, perching primly.

"Glad to see you're keeping yourself in shape," says Mo.

"It's only been two days, I'm hardly likely to have gone to seed."

"True," says Mo, reaching forwards to pat her legging-covered thigh. "I've seen you in the gym, I bet you could burst a volleyball between those thighs. Am I right?"

Kitty crosses her arms. "What's the good news, Mo?"

Mo licks his lips. "That blood in my mouth has made me thirsty. Do you have anything to drink? How about a whiskey?"

Kitty counts to ten as she rises and splashes amber liquid into a glass.

"You can't believe how painful it was for me to replace

you with Abi Minto. There is no freakin' way she's as hot as you are," says Mo. "I actually think her ass is on the fat side."

Kitty can sense his gaze on her backside and legs.

"Just one cube of ice for me. And please, have one yourself," says Mo. "Let's get comfy."

She pours a second drink. She imagines cramming Mo's mouth with ice cubes and then ramming them and broken teeth down his throat with the whiskey bottle. She realises how dangerous this mental image could be too late as a ripple of pleasure runs through her body. The penumbran is moving closer. She spins around. Thinks she glimpses a shadow moving across the floor towards the sofa.

Mo is saying something to her but the adrenalin coursing through her body reduces his words to static.

"Mo, stand up. Now."

He's smiling, patting the sofa, talking about a new project: an erotic thriller that would be *just right* for her.

"Stand the fuck up, now!" she yells at him.

Her words are delivered so feverishly that he actually obeys her, lurching to his feet, a startled look on his face.

It's too late.

The penumbran rises behind him like a balloon being inflated. Something is happening to its right hand. It's changing shape, becoming a set of shears. Mo realises he's no longer the only guest in the room and turns to face the shadow. One moment he is staring wide-eyed and open-mouthed at the penumbran, the next his head is rolling from his shoulders and bouncing across the floor, coming to rest at Kitty's feet, looking up at her with that same expression of incomprehension. His corpse remains standing for a few heartbeats; heartbeats that send spurts of arterial blood arcing from the cleanly severed neck to decorate the coffee table and carpet with Jackson Pollock dashes of crimson, before it tumbles sideways, thumping onto the floor and continuing to pump blood with slowly diminishing vigour.

The penumbran smiles at her and cranes its neck forward, a gesture that says: *Did I do good?*

Kitty can't form any words. She's struggling to even form a coherent thought. Mo's face continues to stare up at her. There's a blob of blood on one of her box-fresh white trainers. She bends to wipe it away but then realises just how close this would bring her to Mo's head. She lets out a whimper and scrubs at the blood with the toe of her other trainer. All she does is smear it across both shoes. She takes a step back from the head.

"What have you done?" she says, her voice quiet. She's not sure if she's talking to herself, or her shadow, or if that amounts to the same thing.

"What. Have. You. Done?" This time the words are shouted.

The penumbran flinches, a look that could be confusion rippling across its face. The monstrous shears in place of its right hand wither to a blob of matter and then a dark copy of her own hand.

"Oh my god, oh my god, oh my god. My life is over. Fucking *over!*" She lurches towards the penumbran, her anger at the situation suddenly outweighing her fear of the creature now bobbing its head in supplication before her.

She points down at Mo's corpse. "I didn't ask you to do that. What am I going to do now? Tell the cops my shadow did it, eh? You've reduced my life to two choices: life in prison or life in an asylum."

I have to hide the body, she thinks. *I have to get rid of all the clues.* She looks at the blood on her shoes. Mo's head still staring at the ceiling. The glasses filled with whiskey and ice. Blood stains everywhere. And his body. His great big body. She plants her face in her hands and lets the tears come. There's no way she can get rid of the body. *It's all over.*

She peels her hands from her eyes when she hears a dragging sound. The penumbran has grabbed Mo's corpse by one hand and is dragging it into the bathroom. As it does so, its right hand transforms again, this time into a short saw with ferocious teeth. The door closes behind it and Kitty hears the body being hefted into the tub. Then the sawing starts. A harsh, purposeful, rasping sound that raises every hair on her body. She grabs one whiskey and downs it, chasing it with the second. The burn brings tears to her eyes. She takes deep breaths. Her heart is throbbing almost painfully. *Is this what it feels like just before you have a heart attack?* She almost laughs at the thought of dying now, and the scene she would leave behind. The stories that would feature in the media for days before it finally became just another mad thing that happened in this mad city, and the only people still interested were the crazies and the occultists.

Her doorbell rings. The most ordinary of sounds amidst the events of this most horrific day. It almost starts her laughing again. She tiptoes across the room, down the corridor, and peers through the spyhole. A police officer is standing outside her door, his face swollen by the fisheye lens.

KITTY PRESSES her face against the door and closes her eyes. *This cannot be happening.* She jerks her face away as the doorbell rings again.

"This is the police. Please open the door."

Kitty takes a step back as the officer thumps the door.

"I can hear activity inside the apartment. I repeat, this is the police, please open up."

Kitty freezes. She just can't process any more options. There's a police officer at her front door and her shadow made flesh in her bathroom, sawing up a corpse. What options could help in a situation like this?

Knuckles bang on wood again. "Police. Open the door."

Please God, not now.

The doorbell. Knuckles. Another call to open the door.

Kitty's survival instincts finally override her paralysis. She realises what she has to do. It's what she always does when life is overwhelming her, what she does best. *You're an actress, for Christ's sake – time to act.*

She tiptoes back along the corridor, pulling off her hoodie so she's just wearing her yoga crop top, spins and strides to the front door. She scrubs her cheeks free of any remaining tears. Takes a deep breath and opens the door, smiling but flustered, a damsel in distress. The police officer is younger than he appeared through the spyhole. He's fresh-faced with unblemished skin and Paul Newman blue eyes. His uniform is immaculate except for a couple of flakes of ash on one shoulder. He smells of smoke.

"Hello officer," she says breathily. "Sorry if you've been knocking for a while, but I'm having some emergency work done in my bathroom. Bit of a biblical flood."

Rasp... Rasp... Rasp...

The sawing continues behind her, and she wills the officer to imagine timber struts or metal pipes being cut to length, rather than a Lebanon-born film director being carved up into portions like a Thanksgiving turkey. The officer's eyes flick down to her chest momentarily and then focus on her face.

"Are you the owner of this property, Katherine Matthews?" he says.

"I am, but everybody calls me Kitty. How can I help you, officer?"

She leaves a gap that he's on the verge of filling when something thuds to the floor in the bathroom. Kitty imagines one of Mo's bloody legs landing on her mock-wooden boards, blood pooling around the faux knots, dribbling along the faux grain. She wants to scream, to run the hell away from this blood-splattered nightmare, but instead she just raises her eyebrows at the officer.

"Workmen, eh?" she says as the sawing starts up again.

Rasp... Rasp... Rasp...

"Indeed," he says.

"You were just about to tell me your name," says Kitty, flapping the front of her crop top as if she was hot. She watches his eyes drop again.

"Officer Sanchez," he says and meets her eyes again.

Now she holds his gaze, not blinking, but throwing thoughts into the back of her eyes. It's acting black magic, the part of her method she can't rationalise or explain, the ability to project – to *radiate* – emotion and energy without any physical change in her expression. Every director she has worked with has praised her for this ability and has tried desperately to determine the secret of her method. The thoughts she projects internally now are the most carnally inappropriate she can conjure in this perilous situation, and she can feel them generating a sexual heat in the space between her and Officer Sanchez. Flushing, he looks down and flicks open his notepad.

His gaze switches quickly between her face and the

page as he reads. "We've received complaints from a neighbour relating to anti-social behaviour relating to this property."

"Anti-social behaviour?" she says, affecting a look of bemusement.

"Allegedly, two nights ago you returned home late in the evening seriously intoxicated, shouting and abusive, whilst accompanied by an unknown male. The following night you disturbed the same neighbour with a loud domestic disturbance." He flips over a page. "They said it sounded like you had locked yourself in the bathroom and were screaming at somebody, possibly a boyfriend, to leave you alone."

"I don't have a boyfriend," she says, leaving the statement hanging.

Officer Sanchez stares at his notepad, glances up at her, and then returns his gaze to the notepad. She has him on the hook.

Another thud from the bathroom. Lighter than before. Kitty imagines one of Mo's arms dropping onto a pile of limbs. It's followed by a squealing sound that sets Kitty's teeth on edge. Maybe it's a belt buckle scraping against acrylic as the penumbran repositions Mo's body. Whatever it is, it stops and the rhythmic sawing starts again.

Rasp... Rasp... Rasp...

"What's he doing in there?"

Kitty takes a deep breath, then allows a shudder of emotion to enter the outward breath. She shakes her head. "Officer Sanchez, I'm sure you see all the world's ills, and so my insignificant problems will seem like nothing to you."

"Ma'am, we all have our crosses to bear. I'm not here to judge, just follow up on a complaint."

"Please call me Kitty. *Ma'am* makes me sound like your mother."

"Okay, Kitty," he says and flushes again.

"Officer Sanchez, this week I was unfairly sacked from my job. That led to a regrettably drunken evening of soul searching and self-pity, and a friend had to bring me home. The following night an ex-boyfriend, who'd physically abused me in our relationship, showed up at my door, tricked his way into the apartment on the pretense of being a changed man, and then reverted to type. I was on the verge of calling the police when he left. And then today, well..." (*Mo's head is brutally cropped from his shoulders, blood fountains from the neck and the head comes to rest at her feet.*)

"Emergency works in the bathroom." Officer Sanchez, now wholly under her spell, completes the list of horrors for her.

Kitty shakes the image of Mo's head from her mind, refocuses her projections onto the officer. "Exactly. Emergency works in the bathroom."

"And decorating," says Officer Sanchez.

"Excuse me?"

He points at her trainers. "You've got paint on your shoes."

Shit. Shit, Shit. Why hadn't she wiped the blood off her trainers?

"Oh yes," says Kitty, her composure crumbling, the energy of her projection waning. She needs him out of here.

"I've never been a fan of red walls myself," he says. "Always felt they were a bit, you know, risqué."

"I guess that's me," says Kitty. "Ms. Risqué."

A silence falls and she makes her final play. She smiles, offering him her crossed wrists, first in front of her, then behind her back, twisting to show him her profile. "Officer Sanchez, if you need to arrest me, so be it. Cuff me however you like. But I promise you there won't be any more complaints. This horror of a week will be behind me soon."

"I don't think there'll be any need for that," he says, returning her smile. He pulls a card from his pocket. "If you have any problems with that ex, you call 911, or call me at the station. In fact, you know, you need anything... you call me."

She takes the card and throws the last of her internal energy at him. It's enough to make him back away, his face red as a schoolboy with a crush on a teacher.

"Thank you, Daniel," she says, reading his name from the card, and that's all she needs to do to send him away smiling.

She closes the door, leans back against it and slides down to the floor. Sweat is running down her back and sides, her breath comes in deep gulps. At the far end of the corridor, the penumbran emerges from the bathroom and heads in the direction of the bedroom. It returns moments later, wheeling one of her largest suitcases and a roll of black trash bags.

Kitty bends forward and lets the sobs come. There's the sound of tearing and then plastic crackles as the bags are filled. Body parts thump into the suitcase, followed by a wet squeezing sound and then the halting progress of a zip sealing the gore inside. She looks up as her shadow wheels the suitcase along the corridor towards her.

"What are you doing?" she hisses. "You can't take it out now. It's too early. Too many people. You have to wait, like... a few hours."

The penumbran's shoulders sag and it turns and traipses back to the living room. *It's like a psychotic toddler*,

Kitty thinks, then quickly buries the thought under others. She can't let it know what she's thinking, what she is already planning. She has to keep herself busy, to focus on something else until she's ready to make her move. She has to keep acting.

Cleaning. That can be my focus. She can immerse herself in that and keep her plan and her fear buried safely beneath thoughts of buckets, cleaning fluids and cloths.

The penumbran follows her into the kitchen, reaching out to stroke her back.

"There's no time for that," she says. "I have to clean up your mess."

She pulls on pink rubber gloves, fills a bucket with soapy water and surveys the living room. There's blood everywhere; soaking into the carpet and sofa, curving lines across occasional tables and the very expensive reclaimed-wood coffee table she'd bought from Anthropologie. Even splashes on the ceiling. *This is going to get messy.* She strips to prevent getting any more incriminating evidence on her clothes and sets to work.

The penumbran squats at the edge of the room, watching her, a needy, attention-seeking expression on its face. She ignores it as much as she can but feels its gaze on her like an icy touch. Bloody suds foam in the carpet beneath her scrubbing and she tries not to picture Mo's head being cropped from his shoulders. She rings out cloths into the bucket. Pink water. Bloody bubbles. She empties it and starts again. The stains are deep into the carpet. She's sweating heavily, but this is good distracting work, and she cleans everything deeply.

She moves to the bathroom. Beneath spotlights, against white tiles, the puddles of blood appear shockingly red. She glimpses her body in the mirror and looks away; hair matted to her forehead, pink stains, dribbles and bubbles marring her skin. The penumbran squats in the doorway, watching.

When she has finished cleaning the bathroom, wiping even the smallest drop of blood from behind the sink and toilet, she showers, scrubbing her body clean of the gruesome work. She knows her cleaning wouldn't defeat a police forensic team; she just has to pray that they never have reason to search her apartment.

Dressing for the outdoors, she ensures she has her cards, phone and keys in her purse. She slips into her pocket a backup credit card that she never normally carries, but keeps her thoughts focused on the disposal of Mo's body. *Don't think about what comes afterwards. Don't think about the plan.*

"Let's go," she says.

She'd tried to move the suitcase herself, but it's just too heavy. The penumbran steps forward and, under its guidance, the suitcase rolls along as if only packed with a couple of T-shirts. It's two o'clock in the morning. There's nobody in the corridor outside Kitty's apartment, nobody in the elevator and nobody in the underground car park. The penumbran lifts the suitcase into the trunk and slides in with it. Kitty closes them inside.

They drive out into the night. Forest fires blaze in the mountains and hills surrounding the city. Some fires have eaten into suburban districts. When she stops at a set of streetlights, flecks of ash settle on the windscreen and hood like shadow snow. A police car rolls to a halt behind Kitty's car and she lets out a little whimper. She wants to jump out and throw herself on the cop's mercy. She wants this nightmare to end. But she's afraid of what the penumbran would do. She cannot have another death on her hands. The cop sounds his horn – two urgent honks. She jumps in her seat and then realises that he's only letting her know the lights have changed to green. She pulls away.

The reservoir is at the edge of the city, but safe from the wildfires. The fire department have cut huge firebreaks into the forest to prevent the pumping stations being damaged. Sadly, a firefighter died during the firebreaks' frantic construction.

Kitty parks her car close to the chain-link fence that rings the reservoir. The night is quiet except for the distant hum of the city and her agitated pulse. She releases her shadow from the trunk of the car and watches as its hand transforms into those fearsome shears and cuts through the fence. The metal pops and pings, coiling and writhing, under the assault. When the gap is large enough for them to fit through, the penumbran lifts the case from the boot and drags it down a steep, scrubby slope to the shoreline.

Using the light of her phone, Kitty searches for big rocks and piles them alongside the suitcase. The penumbran follows her lead. When they have a dozen rocks, all fist-sized or larger, she points at the suitcase. She turns away as the penumbran opens it, releasing an abattoir stench of raw meat. Flesh squelches as it crams the rocks in amidst the portions of Mo's corpse. Kitty hears the zipper seal the contents inside.

"Make sure it goes deep," she says. "Swim out with it."

The penumbran is squatting by the suitcase, peering up at her. She can't see its expression in the darkness, but she senses its suspicion; it tilts its head and doesn't move. She imagines it reaching out to read her mind, icy fingers rummaging through her thoughts.

One. Two. Three. Four. Five. Six. Don't think about what you're going to do. It'll kill you. Seven. Eight. Nine. Ten. Don't think about it.

She stabs a finger at the dark waters. "You made this mess. You fix it. Grab the fucking case, swim out with it, and make sure you don't drop it until you're a long way out. It needs to go deep. And you're strong enough to do it."

The penumbran doesn't move.

One. Two. Three. Four. Five. Six. Seven. Eight. Nine. Ten.

"What are you waiting for?" She lurches forward, hand raised to strike it, at the same time fearing she's gone too far and that she'll provoke a violent response.

But the penumbran flinches, grabs the case by its handle and wades out into the reservoir. The incline is steep, and it's soon swimming, an awkward, one-armed stroke that makes it disappear and reappear from the water with each stroke as its legs send plumes of water into the air. It'd be comic if it wasn't for the circumstances.

One. Two. Three. Four. Five. Wait until it's further out. Six. Seven. Eight. Nine. Ten. Wait. Wait.

The darkness is so profound, and the penumbran so far out, that she now can only see it when the moon catches the spumes of water created by each kick. She calculates the time it will take to swim back versus the time it will take her to reach the car. The splashing stops. She can't see her shadow. When the sound resumes, her penumbran is heading for the shoreline.

"Shit." It's read her thoughts.

She sprints up the slope, the gravel shifting beneath her feet, making it difficult to gain purchase, slowing her up. She can hear splashing sounds approaching the shore. It's too loud. It's too close.

Shit. Shit. Shit.

She stumbles forwards, landing hard, grazing her palm, tearing a hole in the right knee of her jeans. Gets up, takes long strides forwards, trying to devour the distance to the car. Moonlight glints on the cut fence. She's through and fumbling car keys from her pocket. She drops them, bends to grab them.

Jesus, Kitty, this is real life, not a B movie.

The penumbran is on the slope, scrambling up the gravelly incline like a dog chasing a squirrel. Kitty's into the car and stabs the key into the ignition on the third attempt. Her shadow bursts through the fence, flying towards the car, its mouth open wide in a scream of... what? Fear, despair, hate?

She hits the accelerator and speeds away in a cloud of dust and stones, slamming through the gears. The penumbran emerges from the cloud, sprinting after her and, for a few terrible seconds, its thrashing limbs allow it to gain on the car.

"No!" screams Kitty, jumping up a gear and watching the shadow disappear into the night in her rearview mirror.

The pain of separation cuts into her body, a muscular ache that quickly mutates into a bone-deep gnawing as the distance between them grows. She doesn't care. For now, pain equals freedom.

KITTY DRIVES to a cheap motel and pays in cash. Does she really think her shadow will track her payments through credit card payments? She isn't taking the chance. She buys whiskey from a liquor store. She needs to numb the pain of separation. But as she sloshes amber fluid into a plastic cup she found in the bathroom, savouring the peaty aroma as she raises it to her lips, she stops. She can't do this. The pain is her early warning system, her only advantage over the penumbran, and she must endure it to stay alive.

Swearing to herself, she pours the whiskey back into the bottle.

Through a friend, she tracks down a number for Russ Havertz. She calls him, but he doesn't pick up. She leaves a message telling him to call her urgently. She has six missed calls and six messages from her mother. She ignores them.

In the bathroom she pulls off her torn and bloodstained jeans and inspects her wounded knee. It's a mess of grit and dirt pressed into a jagged gash. Wincing, she picks out the grit with a fingernail. Pink water runs down her shin as she washes the wound in the stained tub. She remembers her blood-stained bathroom and the buckets full of pink water spiralling down the plughole. Mo's headless body standing to attention as ribbons of blood spouted from his neck. His severed head peering up at her from the floor. Kitty drops to the floor and vomits into the toilet. It's a long time before she can force herself to stand. She showers, pulls on a threadbare dressing gown and returns to the bedroom.

She calls Russ again. No answer. She leaves another message. *Orders* him to call her *the fuck* back, right away. *I need your help. I'm scared.* She doesn't care that it's the middle of the night. There are no more calls from her mother.

Noisy neighbours sandwich her room. A game show with a screeching audience assaults her through one thin wall. A man babbling into the phone like he's speaking in tongues cuts through the other. A police cruiser with a wailing siren dopplers past. The old air-conditioning unit rattles like an emphysema-addled lung as it drags the smell of the burning mountains into the room.

She sits on the edge of the bed and studies herself in the vanity unit mirror. In a few days she's aged a few years. Her skin is pale and blotchy. Dull eyes stare back at her. They ache as if they've been thumbed deep into her flesh. Another wave of pain saws at her bones and she hugs herself, flopping onto the bed, grinding her teeth, closing her eyes.

Why doesn't she move when she sees the shadow, backlit by sickly yellow streetlights, as it comes to a halt beyond the thin curtains of her room? Why doesn't she scream when it crashes through the window, shards embedded in shadow flesh, hands morphing into serrated spikes, a mouth full of concentric rings of teeth stretching to fill its face as it bends towards her, singing the song of a ringing phone?

She wakes. Doesn't know where she is. Or why she's wearing this tatty dressing gown. It's light outside the room. Then she remembers the reservoir. The chase up the incline. Her knee throbs. Her bones feel broken and glued back together in the wrong sequence. Her phone is ringing and ringing. For a second, she can't remember how to answer a call. She lifts the phone to her ear.

"Hello?" she croaks.

"Jesus, Kitty, you sound terrible."

"Russ?"

"Yes. I've found the Shadow Lady."

"ARE you sure this is the right house?" says Kitty.

She and Russ are sitting in his car, which is parked opposite an ordinary suburban two-story house. Its rectangle of lawn slopes towards a picket fence and a mailbox on a pole. Closed plantation shutters cover the windows. They're closer to the wildfires here. Even though it's the middle of the day, the sky glows an apocalyptic red.

"What were you expecting, the Addams Family mansion?" says Russ, popping open his door.

Russ met Kitty at her motel about an hour after his call, and they'd gone for breakfast at a nearby diner. Kitty found that, despite her pain, she was ravenous. In between mouthfuls of food, her story came pouring out. All of it. She spared Russ none of the details: from how she had chased her shadow away, to her encounter between the sheets and the bloody demise of Mo. She was in a high-stakes game with the penumbran and she only person she could turn to for help was Russ.

When she'd finished, she asked him, "Do you believe me?"

He'd sipped his coffee and stared at her through the steam. "I do."

Kitty tapped her neck. "Because once upon a time a tattoo strangled you?"

"It was a friend," said Russ, unsuccessfully trying to tug the collar of his T-shirt up to hide the scarring around his neck.

Kitty raised an eyebrow.

"Whatever. Let's just say I moved in odd circles for a while and... well, I've seen some weird things." He gestured to the waitress, pulling his wallet from his pocket. "You ready to go?"

She nodded.

The air is heavy with smoke as they walk up the garden path. Kitty covers her mouth with her hand and breathes through her fingers. She knocks on the door. Nobody answers. She waits and tries again. Still no answer.

Russ steps back, cupping hands around his mouth, and calls up to the second-floor windows. "Lisbeth? Are you in there?"

"I'm going round the back," says Kitty.

"Wait—"

Kitty doesn't wait. Cutting across the lawn, she jogs down the path at the side of the house and into a backyard with a pretty stone path winding between ghost gum and totem pole trees. There are flowering shrubs and splashes of colour provided by coneflowers, barberry and silver queen. A bamboo wind chime hangs limp above a sundial pointing to the time with a red-tinted shadow finger. A fine layer of ash covers everything.

The first-floor windows are also covered with plantation shutters. Kitty raps her knuckles on the back door. When nobody answers, she yanks in frustration on its handle. The door is unlocked. She pushes it open.

"Hello?" she calls. "Lisbeth, are you home?"

Russ rounds the corner and stands by her.

"What're you doing?" he says.

"It was unlocked. Don't you think that's weird? The rest of the house is shuttered up like Fort Knox."

"Maybe," says Russ, leaning forwards to peer through the door.

Kitty steps inside. "Lisbeth? I need to speak to you."

"Wait?" says Russ.

She doesn't. Stepping further inside, Kitty finds herself in the well-stocked kitchen of a keen baker. Labelled tubs of various flours, seeds, and decorations are neatly arranged on wooden shelves. Scales, an expensive-looking retro mixer, a bread-maker and piles of cookbooks are scattered over the worktops. For a second, she catches the waft of an unpleasant smell, and then it's sucked through the doorway.

"Not what I was expecting," says Russ, stepping close behind her. "It's more Jane Child than shadow witch."

"Well, Lisbeth makes a mean muffin," says Kitty.

On the opposite side of the room, a corridor leads off into the shadowy interior of the house.

"Lisbeth?" calls Kitty, walking down the corridor. Russ follows her.

There are two more expensively furnished but unremarkable rooms on the first floor. Neither gives the slightest clue as to Lisbeth's esoteric practices.

"Are you sure this is the right address?" says Kitty.

Russ nods. "My source is solid."

A carpeted staircase leads up to the second floor, and a gloomy landing.

"Lisbeth, if you're here, I really need to speak to you."

There's no response.

Kitty looks at Russ, and when he shrugs, she climbs the stairs. The unpleasant smell hits her nostrils again. It's harsh and acrid.

"Jesus," says Russ. "That stinks."

Kitty is halfway up the stairs when the shadow comes screeching towards her. Arms flailing to ward it off, she stumbles back into Russ and then they're tumbling backwards, bumping from wall to bannister and coming to rest in a tangle of limbs at the bottom. On the stairs, a black cat straddling two steps arches its back, fur raised almost perpendicular. It hisses at them, then scrambles over their prone bodies and sprints for the kitchen.

"I've always hated cats," says Kitty, unwinding her legs from Russ'. "You okay?"

"Just my pride that's smarting."

The shock of the cat's attack has removed any remaining sense of caution. Kitty stomps up the stairs, calling out for Lisbeth. She flicks open shutters, bathing the landing in red light to reveal a pile of cat shit as the cause of the stink.

"Somebody forgot to let kitty out," says Russ.

The upstairs comprises three bedrooms and a fourth room that finally confirms they are in the right house. As much as the rest of the interior appears plucked from a website advertising tasteful templates for suburban middle-class homes, Lisbeth's study is furnished direct from scary-booklinedgothiclibraries.com. Where bookshelves don't cover the walls, the dark panelling is decorated with sinister anatomical prints and erotic etchings. Lisbeth's desk is wide, wooden and scarred. The floor is plain boards with a circle of symbols carved at the centre. Within the symbols, dark stains mark the boards.

"Where is she? I need her," says Kitty, actually stamping her foot.

"I'm sorry, Kitty," says Russ.

She reads the spines of books, looking for a reference to shadows, but she can't understand what any of them say. They're Latin or Olde English or a dozen other languages. She pulls volumes from the shelf and leafs through them: dense paragraphs, diagrams of dissected animals, lists of symbols, words on top of words. In a rage of frustration and fear, she hurls a book across the study and then dashes from room to room, calling for Lisbeth. Russ is there, talking to her, trying to calm her, but she can't hear what he's saying. Her bones feel like they might crack. Her head is full of fog.

When she's able to focus again, she's in the backyard, crying disconsolately and clinging on to Russ. He has his arms around her. He's stroking her hair. It feels good.

"We'll keep looking for her," he says. "But tonight, you come back to my place to sleep. Okay?"

"Okay," she mumbles into his chest. She pulls away from him. Scrubs at her face with a sleeve. "I won't sleep with you, you know."

"Don't worry. My husband wouldn't be thrilled if I did that," he says.

AFTER CALLING HOME, Russ drives them to an up-and-coming area of downtown and into the underground car lot beneath a tower of expensive-looking apartments.

"The unions must have done a hell of a job renegotiating grips' wages over the last couple of years, for you to afford a place around here," says Kitty.

"It's a joint investment," says Russ.

They ride the smoothest of elevators to the thirteenth floor and Russ lets them into his apartment. The door opens into a vast living space and kitchen with floor-to-ceiling windows and a wide balcony offering panoramic views of the city. In the distance, Kitty can see the mountains ablaze with forest fires, smoke roiling, helicopters and planes, insect-like specks dropping fire retardants. The sagging belly of a low bank of cloud is stained scarlet.

"She's here," he calls out.

A tall, square-jawed man with dark eyes and a gravity-defying quiff walks into the living room. He looks every inch the movie star.

"Hello Kitty," he says, smiling.

It takes Kitty a few seconds to process who he is. This isn't someone who just *looks* like a movie star, this *is* a movie star. A movie star she has worked with: Bobby Dillard, breakout star of *Jump Cut* and (inevitably) *Jump Cut 2: The Second Cut is the Deepest*. She looks back and forth between Bobby and Russ.

"Yes," says Russ. "We're married."

Laughing, she throws her arms around Bobby. She'd had

a small part on *Jump Cut* and, despite his rising stardom, Bobby had been kind and supportive to every member of the cast. They'd kept in touch after the film wrapped and, if she was honest with herself, she'd been a little in love with him ever since she first met him.

"Awkward," she says, stepping back.

"Why?" he says.

"My relentless flirting."

"Don't worry, it happens to him all the time," says Russ. "I'm fixing margaritas. We need them. And they are *not* optional."

He disappears into the kitchen, accompanied by the sound of clinking glasses and rattling ice cubes.

Bobby shows Kitty to the sofa. "Come on, sit. It sounds like you've had a hell of a time the last few days."

As she drops into the sofa's embrace, Kitty's eyes fill with tears. Russ' kindness, and now the appearance of Bobby, fill her with overwhelming relief. Suddenly, she doesn't feel alone. She wipes away tears, but they keep on coming, soon followed by huge, wracking sobs. Bobby leans over, pulls her against him and hugs her tightly.

"That's it. Let it out," he says.

Blotchy-faced and snotty, she finally brings her sobbing under control. Bobby gives her a tissue, and she blows her nose.

"Better?"

She nods. Even the pain of separation seems more bearable now she is with friends.

"Why didn't you just tell me you were gay?" says Kitty.

Bobby sighs. "Sad and frustrating as it is, and maybe as cowardly as I am, it just wouldn't play well with some of my fanbase."

"He doesn't feel famous, or rich enough, to come out to

the movie world yet," says Russ, entering the living room, expertly carrying three margaritas in alluringly frosted glasses. "Anyway, you're not here to hear homosexual horrors, you're here for respite from battling your supernaturally separated shadow."

"Did you catch that alliteration?" says Bobby. "Russ fancies himself as a screenwriter."

"Bobby's just jealous of my way with words," says Russ. "Anyway, as a start to your recovery process, Doctor Russell prescribes a course of margaritas, one to be taken at least every thirty minutes."

Russ is true to his words, and refill margaritas appear whenever a glass runs dry. While they drink, they prepare a meal. Bobby, wearing a Bart Simpson apron, is head chef. He delegates vegetable-chopping duties to Kitty and he and his husband laugh at her inexpert knife skills. When a second Band-Aid has to be applied to the same finger, Russ steps in and Kitty is told to sit on a bar stool and drink while Bobby questions her about her meeting with Lisbeth, and the penumbran.

Over dinner, James Brown playing in the background, both Bobby and Russ share stories of their own encounters with the supernatural, unnatural and weird. Violent tattoos that can move when you're not looking at them. A friend whose body was occupied by another soul. The English film director, Martin Lavender, who could read your thoughts when he wore a pair of glasses with strangely iridescent lenses.

"I thought I was going mad," said Kitty.

"Those who refuse to accept the possibility of the supernatural are the mad ones," says Bobby. "This city is so *riddled* with the supernatural some people just don't see it anymore."

"Here's to our superb, supernaturally saturated city!" says Russ, raising his margarita. They all clink glasses.

By now Kitty is drunk, and for the first time since she fled the reservoir, the pain of separation has almost disappeared. Alcohol and friends; maybe this is how she can cope with the problem of separation: a perpetual diet of margaritas and champagne. She pictures writing out a diet plan of nothing but booze, and laughter rises through her like bubbles from the bottom of a champagne flute. It starts as a stifled titter, mutates into a barked guffaw and ends with her unable to take a breath for the laughter. When Bobby and Russ are drawn in, this only makes her double down, and soon they're all helplessly pointing at each other as each new wave takes hold.

Suddenly, James Brown is silenced. All the lights go out. The silence and sudden darkness are like a bucket of cold water thrown over Kitty. "What's happening?" she says, pushing back her seat and standing.

Bobby and Russ groan in unison.

"Not again," says Bobby.

"It's just another power cut," says Russ. "It's the forest fires. Third time this week. We're used to it."

"Something to do with substations, or something like that."

Bobby is already up and moving around the room, lighting candles. He sets a candle at the centre of the dinner table, its amber glow illuminating the mess of dirty dishes and glasses.

Russ walks onto the balcony and leans out, looking left and right. "That's irritating. It's just us tonight. All the neighbouring towers still have their power. I told you we should have bought in Tower A."

Kitty grabs the back of her chair. Suddenly she feels totally wasted. Happy wasted. She feels good. Too good.

There's a knock at the front door.

"Probably our friend Margery wanting to borrow candles, again," says Russ, heading for the door, holding a candle on a saucer.

"Are you okay?" says Bobby, taking Kitty's arm.

She smiles, "Just a bit drunk."

Kitty hears the front door open. Russ is speaking to somebody, but she can't hear what they are saying. Then he raises his voice to call, "Kitty, you better come here. This woman says she's your mother."

KITTY'S HEAD is swimming in pleasure. She feels high and drunk and giddy. She can't form thoughts amidst the froth of emotion.

My mother? Here?

The room seems to tilt, and she's staggering towards the front door. Russ stands with one arm across the open door, preventing the woman outside from entering. His other hand raises the candle to bathe the woman's face in an orange glow. At first, Kitty thinks this bedraggled wretch cannot be her mother. She would never allow herself to be seen in this state. Hair plastered to her head with sweat, clothes ripped, make-up almost as bad as Heath Ledger's Joker.

"Kitty, it's me," the woman says.

Kitty looks down at the woman's feet. No expensive, towering heels; bare feet. Muddy and bloody. Broken nails and ruined pedicure. With effort, Kitty swings her gaze back up to the woman's face. It *is* her mother, but her mother *transformed*. Her eyes, usually as hard, cold and clear as ice, are red raw from weeping.

"Mom," says Kitty.

"Shall I let her in?" asks Russ, looking over his shoulder at Kitty.

She nods. Russ removes his arm and Moira shuffles inside. She's carrying a cylindrical hat box. She stretches out her arms, offering it to Kitty.

"He made me bring it to you," says Moira. "You have to take it. Please, take it."

Kitty accepts the box. Its heaviness surprises her. Something moves inside as she tips it. Fluid drips from a corner onto her bare foot. She can't see what it is in the candle's glow.

"Who made you bring it?" she says.

"Gerald. Your stepfather." Moira's voice drops to a broken whisper. "He's come back to punish me for what I did."

"He's dead." Kitty shakes her head. Just the mention of her stepfather is enough to help cut through the fog clouding her brain.

"He's back," says Moira, shaking her head as tears roll down her cheeks.

"What's in the box?" asks Kitty.

"He made me bring it."

"Tell me."

"I can't say. Don't make me say." Moira leans against the wall and slowly slides down, leaving dark streaks that could be mud or blood.

"Kitty, what the hell's going on?" asks Russ.

She shakes her head. "I don't know."

. . .

KITTY LEVERS OFF THE LID, releasing the smell of meat and blood. She grabs Russ' arm to move the candle closer, and stares down at Lisbeth's face, her severed head, mouth open in a silent scream.

"Jesus Christ," says Russ, backing away.

A tremendous surge of pleasure runs through Kitty, and she realises the enormity of her stupidity. It's not the alcohol releasing these feelings within her. It's the proximity of the penumbran. It's found her. How could she have been so dumb as to think she could escape it so easily? A second wave of intense relief runs through her, her bones singing at their release from pain. It's here – now. She drops the box, hearing Lisbeth's head bump across the carpet, then she spins and dashes into the living room. Her shadow is clambering onto the balcony, one hand a huge set of shears.

"Bobby! Get away from the windows!" she screams.

Bobby ignores her warning, turning to face the threat. The shadow surges forward with liquid movements, its arm with shears extending, snaking forward to decapitate him.

Kitty tries to scream, desperately needs the release that the piercing sound will bring, but all she can summon is a strangled cry. Her rage and agony are caught in her diaphragm like a fly in a web. Russ appears by her side, his face twisted into something almost unhuman by the gyre of emotions assailing him. He's repeating *No, no, no,* but he seems unable to take any action once the candlelight reveals the horror before him.

The penumbran has transformed itself. Whereas before it was pure darkness cast in her image, now hanging amidst its shadowy matter is a skeleton suit of grave-dirty bones: skull, clavicle, scapula, sternum, spine, ulna, femur and fibula. Kitty's in no doubt whose bones these are. Metal plates and pins hold together the right fibula. She can picture Gerald's limp. She'd frequently fantasied about breaking his other leg.

With a roar, Russ launches himself at the shadow. Kitty tries to hold him back, but he's too strong, too solid. The penumbran bends like a flame in the wind to avoid his attack and plunges the shears into his back. Kitty sees the point extending from Russ' chest like a huge black thorn above his heart. The penumbran drops its arm and Russ' body slides down and thumps to the floor.

"Russ, Russ!" Kitty drops to his side, tries to call him back, but his blood is pooling around his body. He's gone. Like Bobby. Like Mo. Like Lisbeth.

"He's come back to punish me," says Moira, who has picked herself up off the floor and hobbled into the room. "Because of the harm I did to him."

"It's not Gerald," shouts Kitty, rising. "It's my shadow. It's just using his memory to punish me. And you... you did nothing to him. All you did was *harm* your *daughters*. Turned a blind eye to what he did to me, and to Mel. You let him abuse us."

In all the years since the horror of Gerald's nighttime assaults, since she understood how he'd driven Mel to fling herself from a mountain to escape his predation, she'd never forced that truth through her lips. Many times, she'd plucked up the alcohol-fuelled courage to confront her mother with her crimes. But her anger always came out as something else. She could never cross the Rubicon. Now, amidst the growing pile of bodies, knowing that she herself was likely to die in the following seconds, the words were free.

Moira's face crumples, and a sob escapes her. "I know I failed you. I do. I tried. What I did was too late."

"You did nothing!" Kitty screams.

Moira smiles. It is an expression devoid of any warmth. "I murdered him."

"No. He died of a heart attack."

"After Mel. After he started... what came next. With you. I couldn't allow fear to beat me anymore. I found a woman, a witch, called Lisbeth Kyteler. I paid her, and she cursed him to be eaten alive by his own nightmares. That's why his heart gave out. Lisbeth didn't want to do it. She said it was a powerful curse and it might have repercussions for her in the future. Curses are circular, she said. But I offered her a lot of money. That's why we struggled after Gerald died. It didn't change what had happened to Mel, or you. But it stopped more of it. Kitty, it stopped you falling from a mountain."

Kitty stares at her mother, struggling to process what she has just been told. Struggling to trust her words. But why should she lie now, trapped as they are by this monstrosity born out of Gerald's evil? Her heart tells her this has to be the truth. She remembers how quickly Gerald died.

Moira killed Gerald to protect her.

Kitty sees the truth in this.

Bones moving within its shadow matter, the penumbran stalks towards Moira, raising its shears.

Moira stares at the creature, spits at it, offers up her throat. "I'm not afraid of you now, you bastard."

"Leave her!" shouts Kitty, but the penumbran ignores her.

One, two, three strides and the blades of the shears are closing on exposed flesh. But in those three strides, Kitty has grabbed a broad-bladed carving knife from the kitchen counter. She holds it to her throat, pushing it so close it slices into her flesh.

"You touch her, I'll cut my throat, and that'll end you and me both," she yells.

The penumbran twists its head towards her, Gerald's eyeless skull belatedly following the movement, like a ball suspended in a thick fluid. Its shears-hand, dark matter decorated with yellowed metacarpals and phalanges, closes around Moira's throat.

"I'll do it!" yells Kitty.

The skull stares at her, the standoff stretching to tens of seconds, and then the shears press into Moira's neck.

"Well, fuck you!" Kitty saws into her flesh, and blood runs down her throat. The shears halt their motion. They stare at each other – woman and shadow skeleton.

Slowly, the penumbran withdraws the shears and the terrible blades shrink to become a replica of Kitty's hand. It shudders violently and Gerald's bones fly free of its dark matter, clattering to the floor. Finger bones skitter and click. Gerald's skull shatters into several pieces. The penumbran has returned to its pure shadow self. It walks towards Kitty, its expression wretched. When it stands before her, it mouths a single word: *Please.*

Kitty shakes her head. "Leave, now. If I ever see you again, I'll kill myself."

Shadow tears roll down the penumbran's face as it reaches out a hand to stroke her cheek, but she pulls away from its touch.

"Get the hell out of here," she says.

It lurches away from her, its mouth wide with grief, dashing onto the balcony. Arms spread wide, it launches itself into the blackness like a great dark bird, and Kitty welcomes the return of pain.

MOIRA,

I'm not going to tell you where I am now. I can't take the chance that it might find out... but it's somewhere hot and very exotic on the opposite side of the world. I've changed my name, hair, and even my nationality (it's amazing how easy it is to get a fake passport here). When you practice a foreign accent for long enough, you get used to it.

Where I am has an extradition treaty with home, and I know the police will still be hunting me (Psycho-Head-Collector-Horror-Actress, I believe the Enquirer called me!!) and so I have to be careful. Please burn this after you've read it.

I've been seeing a counsellor – she's broad-minded, but I'm sure she thinks I'm talking in metaphors or whatever, when I talk about the penumbran. Maybe I am. But it helps. I realise now I'll never escape what happened to me. I can't make it go away, become unreal. It happened. To all of us. You, me and Mel. But I don't have to let it control me. I can take back control of my life.

I think that was what the penumbran was. The part of me that would never let go of what happened. The part of me that wants to burn down the world because of it.

It's still out there. It came close to finding me once. I'm good at tuning out the pain now – it's like a radio station playing in the background, and it's only now and then that it's almost too much for me. If I'm ill, or on those days when the black moods overwhelm me. But the pain was always there until one day it wasn't. It must have been so close. I packed and moved on. Left all my new friends behind, just like that. I didn't want them to end up like Russ and Bobby.

That was over a year ago. Maybe it has given up. Or faded away. Maybe it's over.

Mom, I want you to know that I forgive you. It's important that you know that.

Please burn this letter.

Kx

THE CAVE IS high on the side of the mountain, its entrance covered by scrubby bushes with bright thorns. Once, animals used it for shelter and to raise cubs. There are piles of small bones in a recess at the back. But no animals come here now. The cave is empty. Empty, except for darkness and the brooding shadow. When it first came to the cave, the shadow held the form of a beautiful young woman. Over the years, it has changed. It has forgotten the form it once mirrored, slowly transforming, the only features in its smooth face parallel grooves worn into it by a steady flow of tears from eyes that no longer exist.

THE MAN WITH STICKS AND HOOKS

Bella breathes deeply and frowns. She may not see the city rising around her, but she can smell it, taste and feel it with a sensitivity that sighted people cannot. She breathes in again, then sticks out her tongue. The air tastes... *bad*. No, *not* bad, something else. She prides herself on the precision of her vocabulary, her ability to precisely describe her heightened sensory dimension, but today words fail her. Bad isn't the adjective she needs, but search as she might, she cannot find an accurate one.

Her routine hasn't varied this morning. She left her apartment, listening to every ticking tumbler in the lock as she secured her door, and counted the steps to the elevator. Ran her fingertips over buttons from eight to one. She could feel the grease from other fingers. Some days she fancied she could even make out their fingerprints, raised whorls like the most delicate of ammonites. Cables whined as the elevator climbed to her summons. Its interior smelt deliciously of cologne and leather; her neighbour Adam must have left a short while before her; she could almost hear the echoes of his leather briefcase squeaking as he squeezed it beneath a muscular arm. Of course, she's never seen his muscular arms, but she has felt them, she has felt all of his flesh. He comes to her when she calls. Most people do. At ground level, she crossed the atrium, steps echoing around the marble-lined space, and exited the building, the door held open for her by the doorman, Gerard.

The city's morning symphony surrounded her. Engines and horns, snatched conversations, phones trilling, heels clicking and clacking on sidewalks, perfume and diesel and pollen and the almost sweet stench of refuse, the subway rumbling the pavement beneath her feet; the sensation rising into her calves.

Gerard said, as he always said, "Have a good day, Ms. Kirkman."

"*Bella*," she replied admonishingly, as she always replied.

"Have a good day... *Bella*," he said, and she heard the desire in his voice and felt his greedy gaze on her body like fingertips. As usual, she stood there a couple of seconds longer than necessary, letting the power of her physical geometry work on him.

It was their daily ritual.

But now the ritual stops. Instead of starting her walk to the office, she pauses, listening to, smelling and tasting the city. Amidst all the familiar smells is that single, bad (*no, bad really isn't the right adjective*) note.

"Everything okay, Ms... Bella?" says Gerard. He sounds embarrassed to break from the ritual exchange.

She nods her thanks, irritated that he has interrupted her thoughts, and strides away, counting steps, her white cane flicking out ahead of her like a serpent's tongue tasting the air.

The feeling that something is wrong in the city persists.

A voice whispers to her that today won't be a good day for Bella Kirkman. She shakes her head, trying to chase away this nonsense. It clings to her. But bad days don't scare Bella. When, aged six, somebody draws a curtain across the visual world and you're diagnosed with MUVL – Medically Unexplained Visual Loss – with no treatment, no cure, no real answers on offer, you can succumb to fear and withdraw, or you can fight and engage. She chose the latter. She fervently believes any obstacle can be overcome and tells people so daily. When you run a global business, your faith needs to be unshakeable.

The closer she gets to her office, the worse the foul smell becomes. She counts off the blocks. Senses the variations in wind strength against her flesh as she crosses junctions. Normally she luxuriates in the heavenly odours escaping the bakery five minutes from her office, but today they are tainted. The sweet smell of spring blossom from the park is made overripe. Pollen assaults her. She sneezes. Sneezes again. Takes a deep breath and the *bad* smell lodges at the back of her throat. Snatches of anxious conversations buzz around her like insects. The rumble of the subway has worked its way through her entire body. Sweat trickles down her back and sides. People flow around her. The smell is becoming more intense.

She needs coffee. Needs to clean her palate. Just before she reaches her office, she turns into a side street, counting the steps and following her nose to the independent coffee shop – *New You, New Brew* – she always frequents. Mixed in with the heady coffee smell is the essence of the *bad* smell, hard and sharp as a blade. The closer the coffee shop, the worse the smell. Her heart is racing as if she's spent thirty minutes on a treadmill. Her shirt sticks to her in broad patches. Suddenly she feels faint.

She's standing outside the coffee shop. It's here. The *bad* smell is here.

And then... she *sees* it.

Sees...

Sees *him, inside the coffee shop.*

With her *eyes.*

She sees the red man. He's holding yard-long sticks tipped with large hooks, three in each hand, neatly tucked between red fingers tipped with ragged red nails.

As he sees her, his face splits into a leer. Red lips, red gums and red teeth. He works his sticks like a puppeteer and lurches towards her. A red glow emanating from his body highlights details of the coffee shop as he passes through its interior: the edges of tables, a mug piled high with cream and marshmallows, the curve of woman's bare calf, the chequered pattern of floor tiles, the back of a man's jacket and trousers moving ahead of the red man's sticks, all rendered in shades of red.

Bella wants to grasp these fleeting images, to hold and examine them. This is the world she hasn't seen for thirty years. But there is no time. The shop door bursts open and the smell of coffee and cake and the stench of the red man overwhelms her.

The red man works his sticks again. Bella doesn't see the fist. It isn't the red man throwing the punch. Her head snaps around. Sharp pain in her cheek. She's stumbling sideways, falling. Her white cane slips from her grip and skitters across the pavement. A woman screams. A man is yelling from across the road, *"Hey, what the hell, man?"* Hands close around her throat. Hot fingers. Somebody is choking her. The fingers are tight, allowing in no breath. She grabs the hands, feeling buttoned cuffs, the end of jacket sleeves, a wedding band. Tries to peel away the fingers. The grip is immovable. Her pulse roars in her ears. She's choking. She's dying.

The red man comes into view, leaning over her. He has a short beard that rises high on his cheeks. His arms out wide, his sticks moving with purpose in his fingers. The tip of his red tongue sticks between his teeth as he concentrates on his task.

He's controlling somebody with the sticks. Suddenly, Bella is sure of this. He's controlling somebody and that person is choking me.

"Hey, somebody stop him!" A man shouting. Multiple sets of feet slapping the pavement, speeding towards her

The red man looks over his shoulder and, snarling, flicks his sticks up and away. The fingers release Bella's throat and she drags in deep breaths. She hears footsteps sprinting away from her, others sound like they are in pursuit. Men are shouting, threatening, calling for the cops. A woman's voice asks her if she's okay.

"I'm fine," Bella says, pulling herself free of helping hands and clambering to her feet.

Stretching away from her into the darkness, she sees the ghost of a red trail slowly dissipating. It reminds her of a childhood memory. Cleaning a paintbrush in a jam jar of water. Swirls of red paint released from the bristles, writhing in the water like a djinn, a brief life before it became one with the water.

The red disappears. The red man's trail is gone. Darkness returns. There are voices all around her. She ignores them. She has found the word for the bad smell: evil. The red man is evil. And she can see him.

ED CROUCHES BEHIND THE TALL, cylindrical bins and tries to calm his breathing. He can hear the men coming, the heavy slap of their work boots, their calls of encouragement. They're hunting him. And with good reason.

Ed looks down at his hands. Flexes his fingers. He'd just punched a woman for no good reason and then tried to strangle her in the street. *What have I been doing? What the fuck have I been doing?*

As the footsteps come close, he peers between two bins and watches the brightly-lit rectangle at the end of the alley-way. Two men jog to a stop and crane their necks, looking into the shadows. They're both wearing heavy boots, belts bedecked with tools. One wears a yellow safety helmet pushed back from his forehead. They have broad, honest faces, sun-kissed from outside work. One taps the other on the shoulder, shaking his head, and they jog on.

A surge of vomit almost catches Ed by surprise. He leans forward, avoiding puking all over himself, but still splatters his shoes and the bottoms of his trousers. He picks chunks of half-digested food from his brogues then flops back against the wall, pressing his hands against his face, digging his fingers into his eyes, pushing his eyeballs until light flares and pressure builds up inside his head.

What's happening to me? I'm a good man. A good man.

Is that true? says another voice in his mind.

Ed tries to ignore the voice, but memories of the previous evening emerge from the flaring lights. He doesn't want to relive these memories, but how can he not, after what just happened? His wife, Aisha, emerging from the bathroom, wrapped in a white robe, long black hair still wet from the shower, suggesting he leave the laptop alone, leave the words alone, for just five minutes. Why didn't he just sit down and talk to her?

"Deadline", he'd said to her.

"There's always a work deadline," she'd said. *"But what about your wife's baby deadline?"*

He'd ignored her comments. Why couldn't she understand how ambitious he was? That he didn't have time for her nonsense complaints, and he certainly didn't have time for babies? Tonight, every word that left her lips was like sharp metal jabbing into a tooth cavity. He focused on the screen, on his words, on the article that he just couldn't get right. Words never usually deserted him, but writing this article was like trying to keep smoke in a box.

...and the ritual was a hackneyed affair. Candles were lit, incantations were incanted and runes were drawn onto flesh. The heating was on high, even on this warm spring day, so that all in attendance were soon sweating. I presume it was supposed to represent the heat of hell. Hands were laid upon flesh and, on cue, the subject writhed and talk in tongues. Admittedly, it was a disturbing performance of facial and bodily contortion that must have involved detailed choreography and much practice, but...

Aisha was talking again.

"What now?" he'd said, turning to her.

"I said, don't you want this anymore?" She is on the sofa, tears on her cheeks, her robe thrown wide like an angel's wings, to expose flushed, olive-hued flesh, the tattoo of a rose on her right thigh. "What do the others do that I don't?"

The voice in his head snarls, **The bitch won't let you think. Are you going to stand for that**?

Ed can't remember crossing the space between the table

and the sofa. He just remembers being above her, a fist raised, spitting words into her face.

"I need you to leave me alone. I need to... I need space to think."

Had he actually hit her before he stormed out the apartment?

I wouldn't have done that. I'm a good man. I'm just stressed. Under pressure at work. Once I submit this article, once I have the editor off my back, I can take my foot off the pedal. Spend some time with Aisha. Make it up to her. It's the same with the woman at the coffee shop. Subconscious triggers. Stress. Pressure. The work–life balance. I can pull this back. I can be myself again.

He comes back to the moment. He needs to get to the office. He has a meeting. As he clambers to his feet, he notices a smear of vomit on the toe of his right shoe. He grabs a handkerchief from his pocket and pulls out something cold along with it. He holds it up. It's a silver cross on a silver chain.

You never went home, says the voice. **You found another bed. Took a memento**.

He thinks, *I've never seen this before*, then another memory flickers into life – a dark room, the silhouette of a woman, a knife – and, emitting a sound that might be a sob or a snarl, he wrestles it back into a dark place in his mind.

You were magnificent, says the voice.

———

BELLA WRAPS her palms around her hot cup, willing herself to withstand the heat, then raises it to her lips and sips coffee. Normally, she'd buy her extra-hot flat white and head straight to the office; she likes to be sitting at her desk when her team arrives. Today, her nerves still jangling from the assault, she's stayed in the café, to give herself time to process what happened. To process what she'd *seen*. *See*: it wasn't a verb she had ever expected to use again.

The man with sticks and hooks had been painted in shades of red against the black canvas of her MUVL, the glow emanating from his body highlighting glimpses of the world as he moved through it. His eyes were a pale red, like blood dissolved in milk. The sticks ending in those wicked hooks. He made them dance like he was a puppeteer. Bella knew he hadn't thrown the punch. There had been a man moving just ahead of him, his back revealed by the ruby glow emanating from the red man. *He* had been the assailant. He'd struck her, tried to strangle her, then fled with the red man when passers-by came to her aid.

She replays the scene again and again. It's seared into her dark mind. However horrific the red man is, she can *see* him. It's some sort of miracle. Such is her concentration on reviewing the scene, on hunting for clues or understanding, she's oblivious to *New You, New Brew's* customers and staff flowing around her. She's alone in her head with the man with sticks and hooks.

A chair squeaks against linoleum as it's pulled from beneath her table, one leg nudging her foot, and then creaks slightly as somebody lowers their weight onto it. Bella comes out of her trance as she registers their proximity, and her senses start their analysis of data, filling in the blanks left by her absence of sight. She smells a sweet, citrus perfume. The chair had barely made a sound as the person sat with a controlled movement. This must be a young woman, not heavy, good core strength, probably a yoga fan. The woman places a comforting hand on top of Bella's, displaying over-familiarity. Slim, warm fingers. Some are dusted with fine ground coffee, and one fingertip is sticky, maybe with the residue of a flavoured syrup clumsily pumped into a drink.

"Morning, Rachel," says Bella, irritated by her touch, the implicit *pity* – Bella hates pity. She pulls her hand away.

Rachel laughs lightly, seeming not to register Bella's irritation. "How did you know it's me?"

Bella touches her nose and an ear. "These, and simple deduction."

Rachel frequently serves Bella, and they'd started talking about yoga regularly after Bella arrived one morning with a mat tucked under her arm. The deduction wasn't quite the feat Rachel seemed to think it was, but as always, Bella enjoyed the frisson of valediction when she defeated people's expectations of her conditions.

"I wanted to check that you're okay," says Rachel.

"I'm fine, thank you for asking, Rachel," says Bella.

"You've got a bruise coming on your cheek."

Bella touches her high, Slavic cheekbone. It feels puffy and sore. "I'll put some ice on it when I get to the office."

The chair squeaks as Rachel leans forwards. "Somebody said you're not reporting it to the police?"

"Correct," says Bella, her irritation with this presumptuous girl growing. "I will not waste my time, or police time, on this." It's partly a lie. She knows she cannot think about anything else. Won't be able to think about anything other than what she has seen.

"I've seen the man who attacked you before," says Rachel.

Suddenly, Rachel has Bella's attention. "The others said they hadn't seen him before. That he wasn't a regular."

"He isn't a regular. I only glimpsed him when he, you

know… assaulted you. I was more concerned about you, and—"

"But you've seen him before?"

"When I was on a late shift. He tried to hit on me. He's cute, but he was like, so clearly wearing a wedding ring, and when I pointed it out, he fed me the worst *oh-I'm-so-like-nearly-divorced* sob story I have ever heard and believe me I've heard plenty. It's like if you're a waitress they expect you to have the IQ of a muffin."

"Did you get his name?"

Bella can almost hear Rachel thinking. She wants to shout at her to get her muffin brain into gear, but she forces herself to wait. She's read Rachel before, knows she's one of those women who will only get flustered and even more tangential if you push her.

"He said it, but I really can't remember," Rachel says finally.

Bella grinds her teeth in frustration. She feels the need to leave a mark on this girl who obviously has some sort of fangirl crush on her. "You're not much use to me then, are you?"

"Sorry," says Rachel, sounding utterly crestfallen.

"I have to get to the office," says Bella, pushing back her chair and grabbing her white cane. "I don't suppose the man told you where he worked?"

"Oh, yes," says Rachel brightly, pleased to offer something to help rebuild Bella's faith in her. "I remember that. He's a writer, or journalist. He works on that supernatural magazine – what's it called… *Modern Spirits*. He said their offices were nearby, and he'd take me for a tour."

Bella smiles at Rachel even as she imagines punching the girl. *And you didn't think to mention that after you couldn't remember his name?*

Rachel once told Bella that she has a smile that would melt a battleship. She fancies she can hear the girl's muffin brain melting in its blaze.

———

"FUCK'S SAKE, ED," says Fairchild. "My mother could write an article quicker than you, and she's senile."

"It's a complex piece," says Ed.

Fairchild leans forwards, fixes Ed with his infamous stare. Rheumy eyes, peering out from a fan of deep wrinkles, beneath salt-and-pepper eyebrows that look like unruly pubic hair. "With respect, Ed, this is not *Time* magazine, it's *Modern Spirits*. Every piece is the same: skepticism seasoned with cynical titillation and an avoidance of the fact that these people are charlatans or lunatics or both. Solid sentences, a minimum of adjectives. A beginning followed by a middle followed by an end. Rinse and repeat. Now, if the gig no longer fits, if you have a sudden urge to pen a new *Great Gatsby* or *Gravity's Rainbow* or, I don't know, fucking *Salem's Lot* even, be my guest. Just not on my payroll. Understood?"

"Look, I just—"

Fairchild holds up a finger and leans his bulk back into his chair, leather squeaking and metal grating beneath him. There are dusty framed copies of previous covers of the magazine on the wall behind him. Garish headlines in red ink. Lots of exclamation marks.

"Ed, am I known for my patience?"

Ed shakes his head, and Fairchild speaks again. But Ed doesn't hear him; that other voice, the new voice that only exists in his head, is also speaking.

I'll bet if you cut this fat pig from neck to

groin his steaming, rancid guts would cover the office floor. If you don't have a knife, you could do it with your teeth. Rip him open. Then let him talk about patience.

Fairchild is leaning forwards again. "So, we are clear? End of the day or *au revoir*, Ed."

Ed nods. He hadn't heard, but he got the message.

Coward, says the voice.

Get out of my head, thinks Ed, but the voice just laughs.

Fairchild flicks fingers towards Ed, dismissing him. Ed leaves the glass-walled office without another word and heads to his desk. The main office, a small space crammed with ill-matched secondhand desks and swivel chairs, is busy with the clatter of keyboards and phone calls. Only five people work on the magazine, and the noise they manage to generate always amazes Ed. He sits at his desk and fires up his PC, logging into the network.

The buzzer makes an electronic farting sound to announce a visitor at the downstairs entrance, and Claudine, who sells ad space but specializes in office cynicism, traipses over to the video intercom. She peers at the screen, tilting her head slightly to listen.

"Wait one moment," she says into the intercom, her accent heavily Gallic. She turns to the room. "There's a woman at the door who says that this morning she bumped into a man who works on the magazine, at some coffee shop called *New You, New Brew*. Infantile name if you ask me. She wants to talk to you. Any takers, boys?"

Jesus Christ, how has she found me?

Ed focuses on his computer screen, leaning forwards with a furrowed brow and squinting at words he can't focus on, as if he's studying a new Rosetta Stone.

You have to deal with this bitch.

Ed ignores the voice. He has a pain in his chest. He remembers he needs to breathe, but when he does the breath catches in his throat, forcing out a strangled cough.

"Edward. Of course. She must be one of yours," says Claudine, raising herself on tiptoes to look across the office at him. "She's your type: tall, hot and leggy. I know redheads aren't your usual, but..."

Somebody titters.

Somebody else says, "Anything in a skirt is Eddie's type."

Another person says, "Have you introduced this one to the wife?"

You should have finished her this morning! She's dangerous.

"She's nothing to do with me, okay!" shouts Ed, standing so quickly that he sends his wheely chair shooting back into the desk behind him. He turns, fixing his gaze on each member of the team in turn. Across the room, he sees Fairchild levering his bulk from his chair, a murderous expression on his face.

"Ah, fuck it. I resign!"

Ed strides across the room to the door that leads to the bathroom. It also leads to the fire escape. He depresses the safety handle, steps out onto the open platform. Behind him, he hears Fairchild roaring his name, demanding he comes back. Ed ignores him and hurries down the snaking stairs, each step sending a metallic *clang* echoing into the space between buildings. When he reaches ground level, he turns right and runs down the alley in the direction of the back of the building, away from the entrance and the blind woman.

"HELLO? ARE YOU STILL THERE?" says Bella into the intercom. She's been talking to a woman with a French accent, but now the line has gone dead. She presses the buzzer and keeps her finger on it.

The intercom crackles. "Lady, there's nobody here who knows what you are talking about. Sorry I cannot help." The last word sounds like '*elp*.

"Wait," says Bella. "I know he works there. One of his girlfriends told me. I just want to talk to him. Tell him to come down. Please."

There's no response for a few seconds. Bella thinks she's been cut off, then the intercom clicks again.

"Look lady, you want my advice, forget about him. The man cannot keep it in his pants. All he is interested in is cinq à sept. Whatever he's promised you, he promised a dozen other women. Believe me, he's not worth it."

"Please, I'm begging you, just put him on."

The woman sighs. "I cannot. He resigned about, oh... thirty seconds ago, and walked out. Goodbye, lady."

"Tell me his name. Tell me where he lives. Tell me!"

Bella continues to press the buzzer, but this time nobody answers. She slaps a hand against the wall. She's standing by the front entrance to the building. Either the French woman is lying about the man leaving, or he left by another exit.

She turns left, tapping her white cane against the building, and moves along the street. When she comes to the end of the wall, she finds an alleyway between the building and its neighbour. She feels the flow of air carrying the smell of refuse, decomposing cardboard and urine. And something else; a hint of something worse, an evil smell. She strains her eyes into the darkness, and she sees it for a couple of seconds, no more: the last fading swirls of a red trail.

She sets off after him, taking recklessly quick steps, cane darting to and fro, stretching to identify obstacles and threats. The stench of the alleyway is oppressive. Its high walls dampen the city's sounds. She is alone. A dozen yards in, her left shoulder catches on a pipe or piece of metalwork jutting out from the wall, and she hears fabric tear. She pushes on, maneuvering around a collection of large, circular trashcans. Something furry scuttles across her foot and she jumps away. Her right foot lands in something soft and slippery, causing her leg to shoot out at an angle. She can't keep her balance. She bangs against one of the trashcans and pitches forward, landing on her hands and knees amidst a pile of glutinous muck.

She curses as tears run down her cheeks. She hadn't needed her sight to control her destiny and the people around her. Her blindness had tempered a will of steel that must have already been in her. But now that there is a chance of recovering that sight, all she can imagine is what a woman she could become with that gift restored. How rich and powerful she could become? The frustration of having that snatched away from her is too painful to take.

The echo of her frustrated scream hammers back and forth between the walls.

ED DRAINS his beer and tries to ignore the voice in his head. He's been drinking all day, trying to drown it out, but it just won't shut up. Now it's sometime in the evening. Late evening. He hasn't called home. His phone keeps lighting up with Aisha's name. A little red circle over the phone app shows he has ten voicemails.

You need to kill the blind bitch, says the voice, for the hundredth time. **She knows where you work. She's going to mess up your life.**

Ed shakes his head. "I won't do it."

The bar is sparsely populated, with a news channel barking out from a television high on the wall behind a row of optics, but Ed still speaks loud enough to draw the attention of a young couple who have just sat down a couple of tables away.

You will do what I tell you to do.

Ed shakes his head. "Leave me alone."

Ed, says the voice, taking on a wheedling tone, **I'm your friend. I know what's best for you. I know what you need to do to keep yourself safe. To be the true you. I chose you. We were meant to be together.**

"No."

You know it's true. You remember the moment when I found you. When we became one.

Ed doesn't want to remember; he's fighting the memory. But he's too tired, too drunk, and the memory finally breaches his defences. He sees what he was blind to before.

He had been at an exorcism in the basement of a masonic lodge. It was research for his article. The article he couldn't finish. He remembers his cynicism at the whole theatrical process, all the babble about possession and demons. There had been a man writhing on the floor as a priest chanted in Latin. On and on the ceremony had droned. He'd sweated in the heat. When he'd removed his jacket his shirt clung to him like a lover. The rhythm of the priest's chanting had increased. The possessed man arching like a drawn bow. He'd howled in pain, his body contorting, joints popping as they twisted into unnatural angles. Ed's skin had crawled. He'd leaned forwards, as if the possessed man's performance was a magnet. An ecstatic expression erupted onto the man's face at the point of liberation and Ed experienced sharp pains in his back, like hooks digging into his flesh. He told himself he's been bent over at an unnatural angle for far too long, that was all. But when he'd straightened up, he felt lightheaded, like he might collapse. The room was incredibly hot. All the faces were too close, bulging like balloons gripped by fists at their bases. The formerly possessed man was lying on his back, panting, staring up at Ed. At the time, Ed had thought it was because the man could see his cynicism and feared being exposed. Now he realises the expression on the man's face was one of pity.

Ed presses knuckles into his eyes, but he can't unsee the man's expression. "It's bullshit."

The truth, says the voice. **He was such a poor instrument. I was glad they cast me out. But you will be a righteous instrument. We will do such important work.**

"No," says Ed, slapping his hand against the table. The young couple stand, wary eyes on Ed, and take their drinks to a table on the far side of the room. The young man says something to the bartender who is collecting glasses from tables, who then approaches Ed. She's wearing a black vest top that shows off intricate tattoos covering both arms, her chest and her neck all the way up to her chin. She looks like she's about to drown in ink.

"Mister, you're not going to be a problem, are you? Otherwise, you know—" She nods towards the exit. Her sparkling, dark eyes are surrounded by smoky kohl.

Ed shakes his head. "No, sorry. Bad day at the office."

"Don't take this the wrong way, but I always swear by Ernest Hemingway's advice: *Always do sober what you said you'd do drunk. That will teach you to keep your mouth shut.*" She nods earnestly, holding him momentarily with those dark eyes, as if she has just revealed the secret of life, then moves away, collecting glasses from other tables.

The blind woman will be a danger to us when we start to do our work.

"What... work?" says Ed.

Reaping.

"I'm not doing anything for you. You're not real. You're just in my head."

The voice growls. **Pick up your glass.**

"No."

I said, pick up your glass.

Ed tries to fight the movement, but his arm and hand move independently of his will. His fingers curl round the glass and raise it up like a mirror. He sees the curved reflection of old sports posters on the wall behind him.

I'm going to show you myself, to prove that I am here.

For a moment, all Ed sees are the posters. Then, the red man is there, squatting on the back of the banquette seat, sticks held in his fingers, a smile splitting his hairy face. With a moan of disgust, Ed pushes the table away and lurches to his feet, feeling sick. He drops the glass and shards skate across the floor. He's spinning on the spot, flailing his arms over his shoulders, behind his back.

"That's it, out you go, mister!" says the tattooed bartender, raising the counter hatch and striding confidently towards him. "I warned you."

Ed stops his spinning and looks around the bar. Everybody is staring at him from squeezed-balloon faces, just like at the exorcism. He backs away from the bartender and pushes his way out the door into the warm evening and traffic noises.

Behind him, he can just hear the bartender speaking. The other drinkers laugh at whatever she said.

She's mocking you, says the voice.

"Do you blame her?"

Ed doesn't know where's he going or what he's going to do, but he strides purposefully down the street. He needs to move. He needs to get away from here. Away from everything and everyone. He needs to get away from the red man.

He comes to a sudden halt alongside an alleyway between the bar and the next building. His body is held rigid against his will.

Down there.

"No," says Ed.

Pain flares in his back, as if his skin is ripping, and then his limbs are moving beyond his control. He's nothing but a meat puppet. The red man steers him to the shadows behind a tumble of cardboard boxes stuffed with empty bottles and makes him crouch and wait.

They must learn, says the voice.

After thirty minutes, Ed needs the bathroom. The red man won't let him move. Ed pisses in his trousers. After an hour, he thinks his knee joints will burst apart with the pressure. Still, he is held rigid. Finally, the bar empties and closes. The bartender emerges from a side door with another cardboard box of empties and adds them to the pile.

She stretches towards the stars, tilting her head left and right to ease tight muscles, and pulls a joint from the back pocket of her jeans. She lights it and draws a lungful of smoke. The joint's glow momentarily reveals the dragon tattooed on her neck. It seems to writhe with life.

Now, says the voice.

Ed smashes the bottle he has been clutching ever since he crept into his hiding space and rises from the shadows.

"I'm sorry," he says and, despite straining every sinew to control his body, launches himself at the woman. He clamps a hand over her mouth before she can scream and soon the jagged glass in his hand is red.

When Ed has finished, he sits by the body and weeps.

"What are you, a demon?" he asks.

I am you. You are me. We are we, says the voice.

Ed rolls up into a ball, sobbing, and the voice just laughs.

THE FOLLOWING MORNING, Bella is queuing for her coffee in *New You, New Brew*. She'd followed her usual route from her apartment to the coffee shop, hoping for a hint of the red man, the taint in the air, the red smear of his passing, but there was nothing. She'd lingered at the coffee shop's entrance, turning her head, searching for signs, but only growing increasingly annoyed as people asked her if she needed help to get inside. When a woman tried to take her arm to guide her in, she abandoned her vigil and joined the queue. Coffee was tamped, steam hissed, and heating milk gurgled. Orders passed from the till to those making the drinks with the intensity of an army field surgeon requesting instruments to save a soldier from bleeding out.

Last night, using her screen reader and braille display, Bella had trawled the internet into the early hours, hunting for information about the red man, demons and possession. Frustratingly, the search engine's algorithm kept bringing her back to the same stories, retold or repackaged by different people. There was nothing relevant. Nothing about a blind person's experience of the supernatural other than a handful of stories about blind people seeing ghosts. The red man wasn't a ghost. Something made her sure of this.

So, she made her searches more esoteric and ventured into the wilder fringes of the billions of pages that make up the internet. She was close to abandoning her search when she finally found an account of a blind importer of luxury goods called Ned Kinsale, who'd lived in Boston during the late 19th century. His account told of his encounter with a being he called the Man with Sticks and Hooks, who was *red of skin and evil of nature* and who had *snared and worked a low fellow like a marionette with blood on its hands*. He speculated that the Man with Sticks and Hooks could have been a demon. Frustratingly, there was little more detail, and no thoughts on why this blind man had actually been able to see the creature. The screen reader selected a drawing and read its alt tag to Bella: *Drawing based on Ned Kinsale's description. Red man with a heavy beard holding sticks with hooks digging into the back of a peddler*. She burrowed deeper into the web, found more references to the red man, and finally an accurate picture of him had appeared.

The queue moves forward, and a familiar voice says: "Hey, Bella! How're you doing today?"

"I'm fine. My usual please, Rachel."

Rachel fires the order over her shoulder. Bella already

has her debit card in her hand and Rachel taps the machine against it. "All done. You have an amazing day."

When Bella exits the coffee shop, she comes to a sudden halt. The air is thick with the stench of the red man. She scans her surroundings and sees a swirl of red dissipating about twenty yards away from her.

He's close, watching her. A thrill runs through her. He's stalking her. He knows she can see him; that's why he had his puppet attack her. Now he needs to know who she is and where she lives. It's perfect. She can't find the journalist, but that no longer matters. Her red man, the Man with Sticks and Hooks, is coming for her and she has a welcome to prepare.

THE VOICE FORCES Ed to follow the red-haired woman to her office and then to wait, squatting in the shade of trees in the park opposite her building. The hours pass quickly. It feels to Ed that he is occupying a smaller part of his own head now. As if the voice is a swelling tumour slowly pushing him into a corner.

When the woman leaves at six, he follows her. The voice snarls and snaps in his head. It's frustrated. There are too many people. No way to take her without being seen. So, they follow her, keeping their distance, although Ed can't help thinking there's something in the way she holds herself that shows she knows she's being followed. Her home is within an expensive-looking tower block with a doorman and security cameras. The voice snarls again and Ed finds his body jerking into another alleyway and squatting amidst the refuse.

He sniffs his body. He stinks of sweat and piss. He

thinks of Aisha at home, worrying and cursing him. Has she called around hospitals looking for him? Called the police? The voice made him smash his phone. Will he ever see her again?

No, says the voice, laughing. **You are married to me now**.

Then, looking up at the apartment building, Ed sees the woman standing on a balcony with a glass of wine in her hand. He counts the floors to her level. Notes the orientation of her apartment.

Good boy, says the voice. **Now we wait.**

Darkness falls. Still, he waits. The moon stares down at him. The city slips into its dormant state, serenaded by a lullaby of police sirens, screams and drunken shouts. Now the streets are populated by the night people: the homeless, the drunk, the poor, the mad and the predators.

Like you, says the voice, and Ed's body jerks into life.

He crosses the road and finds his way to the rear of the building. Where only a day before he had fought against the possession (*yes*, he tells himself; *I accept I am possessed*, ignoring the voice's laughter) now he feels like a passenger in his own flesh. *I am no longer* he; *I am* they, he thinks.

That's the spirit, says the voice.

They break a window and clamber into a storeroom. Their hand drips blood. Their body leans forwards and moves with a predatory sway through dim corridors. They find an internal fire stairwell. Harsh lights. Bare concrete walls and steps. The smell of fresh paint. Cold metal handrail. They climb, counting off the floors, following the echoing steps, until they reach the level where the red-haired woman lives.

They push through a door with the floor number

painted on it, instantly replacing the cold austerity of the stairwell with the rich indulgence of the living areas. The corridor walls are covered with ochre wallpaper and ornamented with large, abstract paintings. Towering rubber plants spread glossy leaves next to the elevator doors and at other points along the corridor with its polished parquet floor. The air-conditioning hum is almost subliminal. The space smells subtly of lemons and spices.

Halfway down the corridor, an apartment door stands ajar.

She knows we're here, says the voice.

"How can she?" asks Ed.

For the first time, the voice does not respond to his question, and just jerks their body towards the door. They peer in through the opening. It's dark inside. No need for a blind person to switch on the lights.

They reach inside the doorway, palm patting the wall, and find a light switch. They flick it on and bathe the apartment's entrance corridor in light. There's no movement. They slip inside and close the door behind them. The corridor is decorated with an impersonal tastefulness. They move forwards, steps silent on the plush carpet.

I will not kill again, thinks Ed. He tries to exert some control over his legs and for one glorious moment brings his body to a halt.

The voice snarls and Ed's consciousness, that sense of what is still definably him, receives a stunning blow that sends him spinning through a world of white pain. When he finally recovers and his sight returns, he finds his body stalking into the apartment's living area. Here, the floor is covered by thick, clear plastic, the type used to protect carpets whilst decorating. The room is a wide, minimally furnished space fronted by floor-to-ceiling windows and the balcony on which they'd seen the red-haired woman.

She stands at the centre of the room, facing them. Waiting for them. Despite everything that is happening to Ed, his hunger for women is fired by her appearance. She's dressed as if for a date, in a tight, dark green cashmere jumper and skinny jeans, her deep red lips contrasting with her porcelain skin and her red hair tumbling in waves past sparking earrings to her shoulders. Her green eyes stare sightlessly beyond him.

Ed tries to force words through their lips. He wants to warn her, to yell at her, to flee, to run and never stop running, but the red man won't let him. Ed tries to turn their body, to force it out of the apartment and away from the woman. One last act before he is nothing but a flicker of consciousness in an uncontrollable tower of flesh. But his efforts have no effect.

"I can see you," says the woman.

Ed is confused. She's blind. She uses a white cane. He's watched her for an entire day; the way she moved couldn't be an act.

The voice that passes Ed's lips is not his own. "That is why you have to die."

Suddenly, Ed realises what she means and his heart leaps. It's the red man, the man with sticks and hooks that he saw momentarily in his beer glass. It's the thing that's controlling Ed that she can see. Hope flares in him. Maybe she can help free him of this unholy parasite.

"I don't want to die," says the woman, her voice admirably calm. "I want to see. And to see more than your filthy face."

The red man's voice forces itself between their lips

again, first as a thick laugh, then as words. "Charity is the work of angels. I, as you see, am not of that clan."

"That is where you are wrong," says the woman, moving her right hand behind her back. "I work in the world of charity and everybody will tell you I am far from an angel."

The red man emits another gurgling sound.

"And I know you," says the woman. "I know about Ned Kinsale and his Society of the Night hunting you all those years. For a blind man, he was the most dedicated diarist. I believe it was the love of his life, Lizzie Boothe, that actually set down his thoughts. She was one body you took and abandoned. All those bodies you used and abandoned to elude their chase: Archibald Swartz, Bobby Yellowknife, Finnegan O'Rourke. It's a long list. But in the end, you got your man. You butchered Ned Kinsale."

Ed can feel the red man's emotional turmoil like a squall blowing inside his mind. This woman's list of names, her knowledge, has unsettled – even *scared* – the red man. He's nonplussed by his secret history being exposed, made off-balance by her icy calm. Willing the woman to keep up her distraction, Ed gathers all his remaining strength, preparing himself for one mighty push, a final attempt to dislodge this creature from his mind and body.

Then the woman's hand appears from behind her back. She's holding a broad-bladed kitchen knife. *That's it!* He wills her on. *Stab the red man now, while he's distracted.* Instead, she takes two steps forward and plunges the knife into Ed's chest. Shocked, he watches her pull it out, dripping blood, and then plunge it in three more times.

She steps back as he crumples to the plastic-covered floor, fingers pawing his ruined flesh, thick blood pumping between his fingers. *The plastic: she planned this. She planned to murder me.*

"Why?" he says, and then he is gone.

BELLA HAD MEASURED the distance between herself and the puppet she'd just knifed, using his voice and the glow emanating from the body of the man with sticks and hooks. Her four stabs had been deliberately spaced to ensure the maximum chance of puncturing his heart. She needed him dead. Wounded wouldn't do.

Now she watches the red man unhook his sticks from the corpse at his feet. His mouth is a thin, grim line. His eyes are wild, unsure. He's been tricked and now he's fearful, even more dangerous.

"I know you can only survive away from a host for a short time. Once they die, or you leave, or are cast out, you have to move on to a new host." She smiles at him and turns on the spot, opening her arms wide. "Well, here I am. Take me."

Facing away from the red man, she sees nothing but a scarlet glow at the edge of her usual vista of darkness. She waits. Has she misjudged? Can this thing survive away from a host for longer than Kinsale thought? Has it fled to look for a fresh victim? Or has it perished, denied the sustenance of another being to feed on?

When the hooks bite into her flesh, she arches her spine and screams. She drops to her knees. The sensation is so sharp, so penetrating, it exists in the murky hinterland between pleasure and pain.

Is this what you wanted? says the voice.

She shakes her head. "More. Much more," she says. "I need to see, or I will be useless to you."

The voice snarls. **I will not be used.**

"I can't do your will if I can't see," she says.

You tricked me into this.

"Isn't that what weak men always say?"

Another snarl.

And then it happens. Red light floods into her eyes, and she sees her apartment for the first time. Each detail is rendered in shades of red, ruby and scarlet, but every detail is there. She steps out onto the balcony. Tears fill her eyes as she looks up at skyscrapers with their patchworks of lit windows. In the street below, a car rolls by. A cat strolls along the pavement. Lovers kiss beneath a tree. A scarlet world. Her world.

You will do what I say now, says the voice.

"Oh, I don't think our relationship is going to be like your usual ones," Bella says. "It's going to be much more profitable as a partnership."

WE HAVE COME FOR YOUR CHILDREN

A horror story in 333 words

The doorbell rings.

Jenny ignores it. Stares at the iPad screen, willing the word flow to become a story. She should be in a lecture hall at university, but she already knows academia can't help her. So here she is, in her room lined with books, surviving on Cheerios, living in her Scooby Doo onesie, oh-so-close to finishing her - if she does say so herself - amazing first novel, *Jemima & Jacques Lose Tomorrow*.

It's brilliant.

Effing brilliant!

She just knows it.

The doorbell rings again. An irritatingly sustained jangling. She loses the thread of her sentence.

Goddamnit!

She stomps into the hall, and yanks open the door to reveal three shrunken old ladies.

– Oh, hello, says Jenny.

The old ladies giggle, sharing mischievous glances.

God botherers, Jenny thinks.

– Oh no, says the first old lady, screwing up her face.

– Never that, says the second, that's far too *new-fangled*.

– We're here for your children, says the third.

Suddenly, Jenny is stumbling backwards, her head cotton wool, her legs overcooked spaghetti.

White light. Her head hurts. She's on the floor, looking up at three wrinkly faces.

– I don't have any children, she mutters, eyes closing.

– Oh, but you do, chorus the old ladies.

Jenny wakes with her iPad cradled in her hands.

Nightmare.

Dreaming again.

Working too hard, girl.

Maybe she needs to up her sleep from three hours to five a night.

No.

When the novel is finished. She'll sleep then.

Her iPad's asleep. She swipes its screen and keys in her password.

No... no... NO!

Her novel! Where is her novel? She must have deleted it accidentally when she slumped asleep.

Keep calm! You're a diligent writer. You back up *Jemima and Jacques* in the cloud. You may have lost a morning's work, that's all.

She navigates to her cloud account. Opens her folder. There's only one document in it.

She opens it.

A single line of text.

We have Jemima and Jacques. They're safe now. You can't hurt them anymore.

THE MASTER WORKSHOP

I had been resident at Lord Jared Hockenheim's country mansion, Euterpe Hall, for a full three weeks before he granted me the privilege of laying my eyes on one of his near-mythical violins. Heavy rain laced patterns onto the windows, obscuring a view of grand gardens run wild, as I took tea in a reception room in the west wing. The room was furnished with dark, nearly black, furniture of a baroque and most eccentric design in keeping with the rest of the property. Lord Hockenheim had a taste for carvings of purgatory scenes and as one placed a hand on a chair's armrest one felt rib cages, broken limbs or tortured torsos pressing into one's flesh.

Truth be told, at that very moment I was seriously wondering at the wisdom of accepting Hockenheim's invitation. I felt at risk of wasting my youth. But just as I contemplated creating a tale about an elderly, sick relative to allow me to extract myself from the situation, the door squealed open and the old man shuffled into the room, accompanied by his ever-present, consumptive cough.

He was carrying an ornate wooden box, roughly the length of an arm, and he laid this on the occasional table beside me. The dark wood was smooth, unscarred by carving.

He raised a heavy, grey eyebrow. "Open it."

I clicked open two brass clasps and lifted the lid. Inside, lying on a bed of ruby satin, was a violin, a genuine Hockenheim. He manufactured only one of these instruments each year. Even though the afternoon light creeping into the room was weak, the instrument's burnished wood gleamed with a vital lustre. The craftsmanship was flawless. Wood curving with organic grace. Not one joint visible, however closely I scrutinised it. It was truly wonderful. I could barely contain my desire to test the true magic of the instrument and, looking at him with pleading eyes, I picked up a bow.

"May I, sir?" I asked.

He shrugged, and a smile appeared amidst the wrinkles and flaps of sagging skin. I calculated it was only the second time I had ever witnessed the phenomenon, the first occasion being cruel glee at seeing my mud-splattered and dishevelled appearance when I arrived. If the truth be told, it was a most unpleasant smile.

"How shall you ever learn to craft such an instrument if you are ignorant of the beauty it can create?" He released a cough that might have contained a trace of laughter.

I drew the bow across the strings, sliding my fingers through a scale, afraid to squeeze or press too hard. The sounds that I, a promising, but still young, musician could produce almost moved me to tears. It was as if the instrument had access to the human soul or heart and could reproduce in sound what could normally only be experienced in abstract emotions.

"I..." I was lost for words.

Lord Hockenheim grimaced and nodded at the case. Reverently, I returned the instrument to its satin bed.

"Young Master Jackson, a word of warning: do not let your gentle nature interfere with the harsher aspects of our task. The creation of such perfection is not without cost, and the craftsman must pay most of it." He raised his eyebrows, and I nodded in reply. "Take the violin to your room. Begin a relationship with it. Tomorrow we create its sister. We have a commission – from a member of the high aristocracy."

With those words, he struggled to his feet, brittle bones cracking and popping, and shuffled off into the shadows, leaving me to ponder the task ahead.

On the way back to my room, the violin case held before me like an offering to the gods, I again stopped outside the master workshop. When I arrived at Euterpe Hall, Lord Hockenheim's valet had instructed me that I could not enter this room until given permission by the master of the house. The primary workshop on the ground floor, with its benches, vices, chisels and pots of heady varnishes I could enter and use whenever I wished; the master workshop held trade secrets I was presently denied. I suspected that the door to this room would be locked, although I was not inclined to test this assumption and counter my mentor's wishes. I too had my secrets. I would not wish those to be disturbed.

———

DESPITE LORD HOCKENHEIM'S ECCENTRICITIES, I was a very lucky young man. Chosen by the most renowned and reclusive violin maker in the world to be his sole apprentice, a receptacle for all his wisdom, experience and skill; a companion for an eccentric old man who had little time left on this earth.

I could still vividly recall my feelings of shock and pride as I was given the news by the owner of the humble firm whose employment I had enjoyed for five years, a firm of proud artisans that made good, but not great, instruments. It bemused me. What could such a great man as Hockenheim have seen in me? Quickly, I resolved to put aside my own doubts, my hesitant nature, and the nagging fear that the discovery of my unfortunate past might cause an abrupt end to my tutelage – I seized the unique opportunity.

My parents were glad that my fortunes had taken such a dramatic turn for the better, and most of my friends and fellow artisans wished me well, their words tempered by a mixture of awe and disbelief. Only a few scoffed at my decision, casting foul aspersions on the good name of my new mentor, accusing him of using the black arts and a pact with the devil to create his instruments. I dismissed these people as the jealous fools that they were. Within the week, I was riding my horse down an atrocious country track, more akin to a bog than a road, in the middle of a storm of biblical intensity. Although I was glad when my tiring journey came to its end, it must be told that Euterpe Hall was not the most handsome or welcoming building in aspect. But who was I to critique the choices of a genius?

After I had made my fingers sore playing the magical Hockenheim violin, losing track of time and missing dinner, I collapsed into an unruly sleep. Once again, the nightmares came. My instinct was to ascribe them to my still unfamiliar surroundings, but I was worried by the feverish quality of the dreams. Inevitably, my past found root in the fertile soil of these night terrors. I had accepted the fact that I would never be truly free of this yoke. In the nightmare, the pistol was heavy in my right hand. The swirling confusion of sounds around me. Plates smashing. Men shouting. My wife's scream. But I was not in our house, I was standing outside the master workshop and the woman's scream was coming from inside that room. Another noise competed for my attention, the rhythmic squeak of a wheel or handle being turned, and the screams climbed in pitch, the scales of the damned. She was screaming my name. It was so real.

When I awoke with a violent start, tangled between too many heavy blankets, I could not be sure whether *I* had screamed. I prayed that I had not woken Lord Hockenheim. I did not wish him to consider me a weak fool, or somebody who carried darkness inside.

OVER THE COURSE of the next three weeks, we fashioned the body of the violin. Lord Hockenheim demonstrated his technique fastidiously with diagrams and with his hands, and then instructed me to follow his example. He did not spare me the sharp edge of his temper and tongue when I failed to fully execute his directions. He had little patience. Gradually, we made progress, and I gained in confidence, taking on more of the work myself, but always watched by my mentor. When I enquired about the contents of the master workshop, he would ignore the question and withdraw from the room. The secret hung heavy over me.

Lord Hockenheim's health deteriorated during this period. I do not think he was used to working much these days, which restricted us to spending only three hours together each day. Then, one gloomy Monday, when I had failed to grasp a technique and we had argued and made no genuine progress, he informed me that Lady Westerburg, the noblewoman who had commissioned the Hockenheim, was to visit us.

The night before our visitor arrived, I suffered another terrible nightmare that braided past and present to create a hideous tapestry. I pressed my ear against the cold wood of the door to the master workshop and heard every squeak from within the room. I determined it must be a system of pulleys or some similar device. I wondered why there were no screams emanating from the room on this occasion, but as soon as the thought entered my mind, I was aware of the pistol in my hand and a scream ripped through the darkness behind me. I spun and fired in one motion. I saw the bullet exit the muzzle of the pistol, travelling through a slowly spreading billow of smoke, spinning through the air, crashing into my wife's forehead. Splinters of bone. Blood splashing my face.

When I jerked awake, tears covered my face. The burden of guilt had never been as heavy as this, and I was convinced that the intensity of my relationship with Lord Hockenheim and the secrecy attached to the master workshop was affecting my sanity. If I entered the workshop and saw what Lord Hockenheim hid from me so diligently, then I might free myself of this reawakened and terrifying guilt.

So, wrapping myself in a heavy robe, I made my way through the pitch-dark mansion at the centre of a circle of candlelight. I listened for the sound of servants' footfalls, but all was silent. Night revealed the true ugliness of the house during that candlelit journey. The master workshop was in a separate wing of the house to my bedroom and, as I made my way through its strange architecture, full of point-less nooks and crannies, its tortured carvings watching me with blank eyes, a sense of dread crept into my mind. Was I truly being observed? I was glad to arrive at the door of the master workshop, hoping that this would calm my feverish state of mind.

As in my dream, I pressed my ear against the door, but an absolute silence greeted me. I laid a hand on the door handle and pressed down. It was well-oiled and silent, but locked. I was about to return to my room when I heard a gentle chinking sound from within. It sounded like a dangling belt buckle made musical by a gentle breeze. I peered through the keyhole, but there was no light. I returned to my room, through the gloom, beneath the watchful sculptured eyes, and lay pondering the secret room until dawn, when I fell asleep and was late for my session in the Primary Workshop, causing another violent argument.

"LET us toast the world-famous genius, Lord Adolphus Hockenheim, and his handsome young pupil, Master Jackson," said Lady Westerberg, raising a glass of amber wine first to the old man and then to me. Her eyes reflected the candles placed at regular intervals along the length of the dinner table. She was young, exquisitely dressed, and everything about her shone: her green eyes, her pale skin, her bowed lips, the jewels dangling from her ears and resting against her throat. I was making a fool of myself with clumsy attempts at conversation. I had always fallen for women with dizzying ease.

When Lady Westerberg had arrived, Lord Hockenheim

had not been well enough to greet her and so it had fallen to me to guide her to her rooms, escort her on a tour of the house and grounds and show her the complete body of her original Hockenheim; all it required were the strings. She was most pleased by our progress.

"No," said Lord Hockenheim pointedly. "Let us toast the beauty of art, the beauty of music, and most of all the beauty of our guest."

"You are too kind," said Lady Westerberg, with the casual air of one accustomed to such compliments.

"Your beauty is without compare, Lady Westerberg," he croaked, then coughed. "It's a much-acknowledged fact in polite society, I am led to believe."

"I would be pleased if you would consent to call me Anna. It is my much-used name in polite society," she said, laughing lightly.

"Wit and beauty. Anna it shall be. Have you ever seen a lady as beautiful as Anna, Master Jackson?" he asked me with a sly grin. I agreed with his sentiment. To my eyes, Anna seemed touched by the statement. Her smile was enough to raise my pulse.

Lord Hockenheim returned his attention to our guest. "One thing we should always remember, as I never tire of reminding my young apprentice, is that beauty always has a price; the time one spends tending beauty, the money one spends to maintain and augment it with jewellery and fine fabrics, and the fear of losing beauty that gnaws at the soul. There is a cost that accompanies beauty, as there is a cost that accompanies the creation of art."

Our radiant guest appeared politely bemused by this sudden burst of philosophy, an expression that shifted to concern as Lord Hockenheim collapsed into a violent coughing spasm. I stood and made myself ready to help him to his bedroom, as I had done on many previous occasions, but the old man struggled to gain control of his lungs and impatiently waved me back to my seat. He rang a small bell beside his plate and his valet slid into the room with a tray balanced on the flat of his right hand. Upon the tray were three glasses containing a greenish liquid; the valet set one before each of us before disappearing once again. Lord Hockenheim threw back his drink and sighed with relief.

"My favourite liqueur," he said, as his breathing became more controlled.

He indicated with upward curled fingers that we should drink the liqueur before us. Dutifully, we lifted our glasses to our host, then each other, and sipped the heavily scented drink, which tasted of honey and brandy and had a strangely gritty feel to it. I looked at Anna, nodded my head slightly, and we both made noises of appreciation, even though I suspected our guest didn't favour such potent brews.

We let Lord Hockenheim recover fully in silence for a few moments, and then he proceeded in a quieter voice so as not to aggravate the complaint. "As I was saying, before being so rudely interrupted by my rebellious lungs: there is a price to pay when we create art. The higher the price, the greater the sacrifice you make, the greater the resulting art. Of course, the greatest sacrifice is death. When death is part of the equation, the value is... inestimable."

I could see that Lord Hockenheim's continued rumina-tions on art did not agree with our guest. She rubbed her forehead and then her eyes as if she were suffering from a headache. I made to ask if I could help her but discovered I could not move my tongue. It was quite numb. A dead lump of muscle. I turned to face Lord Hockenheim. It was a slow, unsteady manoeuvre. My gaze wavered, as if I was looking into a heat haze. I was losing my balance. My mentor wore one of his rare smiles.

"Therefore, to conclude my argument, we must agree that all the greatest artists are also murderers," he said. "That is why I chose young Master Jackson here, a murderer already, with the makings of a fine artist. Lady Westerberg – sorry, *Anna* – you would not think that this fine, apparently upstanding young man had shot his first wife through the forehead with a pistol, would you? But he is an artist, not a braggart. He knows what to reveal and when."

The world tilted. Anna's eyes closed, and she fell from her chair into the ballooning swell of her skirt. The grit in the liqueurs. A poison? A potent narcotic? How naïve I had been to think my wife's fate would escape his attention. I tried to scream at him: it had been an accident, there had been looters in our house. I was drunk but trying to protect her. She jumped at me from the shadows. Honestly, that was how it happened. The arguments we had before that day, the accusations that I beat her, that the looters were a fabrication – all lies. The guilt and drug were too much. I slid from my chair, landing on my hands and knees. The last thing I saw before unconsciousness claimed me was a door opening and the valet's shiny boots approaching me.

AS CONSCIOUSNESS CRAWLED into my skull, I could hear the steady squeak of a handle or wheel near to my head. I coughed my lungs into working order and a strange mix of aromas assaulted me. The overriding smell was medical; something acrid and heavy, but beneath this was another, altogether more terrifying, smell; like a key it worked on my padlocked memories – it was the smell of meat and blood, the smell of death.

I forced my eyes open, but immediately wished that they had stayed shuttered against the diabolical scene before me. I leant sideways in my chair, my still befuddled brain moving as if it were floating free within my skull, and retched part-digested food and bile onto the stone floor.

Here was the secret of the master workshop that I had so foolishly wished to access. Anna lay on a wooden bench to my left. One of the leather restraining belts that had been used to hold her body had worked loose, and its buckle chinked in a gentle breeze. She was quite dead. Her garments were open from throat to belly and her heart removed with a surgeon's precision.

On the opposite side of my chair was an elaborate device of pulleys, wheels, clamps and counterweights that hung within an ornate wooden framework. At the centre of the machine was a thin strand of glistening fibre. Lord Hockenheim, wearing a long, blood-soaked apron, was turning a handle, slowly stretching the fibre. He turned to me and smiled. He raised my left arm, which was still heavy and uncoordinated from the effects of the narcotic and placed it on the machine's handle. Holding it in place with his own hand, he turned it.

"The human heart," he said, staring into my eyes. "The perfect instrument. Cured, pressed, delicately stretched and dried, it makes the finest strings for violins. It affords the musician direct access to the chords of the soul."

He removed his hand from the handle, leaving mine hanging in place, a slight tingling indicating the return of its mobility.

"I understand you," he said. "Your wife's death was no accident. It was a step on the road to artistry. Admit it."

His skull-like face was close to mine. I could smell his breath, the rot in his guts. He nodded at the handle. What could I do? He understood me. He saw me better than I saw myself. I gritted my teeth, concentrating, and turned the squeaking handle. Lord Hockenheim sighed, then sat on a chair, as if relieved of a great burden.

WHAT I DONE FOR THE DEVIL

Mr Reporter Man, sir, what I'm going to tell you is as real and truthful as these bars between us. It don't matter that people don't believe me. I just need to say why I done so much killing.

You recording this? Good. Phone fully charged? Good, a professional. I like that. Here we go.

I was five years of age when I first met the Devil. It was a hot night, and I could not sleep. No, sir. When I got up to get a glass of lemonade, he was sitting on the end of my bed.

He wasn't no movie devil. No smooth, handsome fellow or goat-man with a pitchfork. He was ordinary looking, with a black suit and a white shirt. They was all crumpled like he'd been sitting in them a long time in an office or something. His black tie was pulled away from his throat. I guess he was hot, too. He looked sad.

He said to me: *I want you to kill your mother and father*.

Now at the time, I didn't know he was the Devil. I thought he was just some pervert like my ma told me about. The kind that does bad things to children. So, I shook my head.

Do you know who I am, he asked.

A wicked man, I said.

A wicked man, he repeated. He laughed for a long time after that. He laughed so much that he cried. And do you know what he cried, Mr Reporter Man? He didn't cry no tears, he cried blood. His face was red as one of them French apples by the time he stopped himself laughing.

I'm the Devil, he said, and used a red handkerchief to wipe his red face.

Now, I seen the blood tears and I know he ain't no normal wicked man. I was beyond scared then, but being a child made me bold.

I can't kill my ma and pa, I said. *I'm adopted. I don't know my real ma and pa.*

I know that, he said, *but these false parents will have to do.*

Why do I have to kill them? I said.

Because I'm the Devil and somebody made a bargain with me. I made him wealthy and famous, and they gave you to me. If you don't kill them, well...

His face was sad again. He shrugged his shoulders, clicked his fingers and the walls of my room disappeared. Behind me was a dark plain. I was standing at the gates of a city that went miles into the dark sky. It was black and cold and dead. My ears nearly burst with all the screams coming out of that city.

My life changed during those few seconds, Mr Reporter Man. You see, after that I had little doubt that he was the Devil himself, just like he had said, and that city was Hell.

He took me to the tool shed and showed me how to make a poison nobody could detect. Next morning, I took breakfast to Ma and Pa in bed, and they never got up.

I see you looking at me with quizzical eyes, Mr Reporter

Man. I know you think I'm saying all this to get myself an insanity verdict, and I don't blame you. All I ask is that you record what I say. Will you do that? Good.

After the funeral, they moved me from family to family. Folks never took a liking to me, which ain't surprising, on account of death following me around. Sometimes I wouldn't see the Devil for six months or a year, but he'd always come back in the end.

Normally, I'd wake up at night and he'd be there sitting on the end of my bed. But once I was sitting on a swing on a porch, touching up a girl I was dating, and suddenly he was right there next to me. Can you believe that? He talked away to me, but she couldn't hear a word. Good thing really, because later that night I tipped her down a well just like he asked me to do.

It got so that I could kill using just about anything and leave no evidence. Poison, knives, cliffs, soil, water – you would not believe the number of ways there is to kill a person dead.

That don't mean nobody suspected me and treated me like I was *born* of the Devil. They did that all right. But none of them could prove a thing. And as long as I was staying out of that city, I was okay. I'd never be *happy*. How could I be *happy* when I was damned to be a murdering son-of-a-bitch all my life? But I was okay, and I would have carried on being okay if it wasn't for one thing, or should I say one *man*. You see, Mr Reporter Man, over the years I learned to hate one man. It wasn't none of the people I killed, and it wasn't the Devil. He was just taking what was his. No, it was the person who used me to make himself rich and famous at my expense.

I decided this person should die. So, when the Devil next appeared, I asked him who he made the bargain with.

He didn't hesitate with his answer. That's one thing I like about the Devil: he never lies.

Your blood father, he said.

Mr Reporter Man, I guess it's true to say I wasn't too shocked by this. I suppose in my mind I must have known all along. I asked him who he was.

Why do you need to know? He replied.

Because I'm going to kill him, I said.

I haven't asked you to kill him.

No, he asked for it himself.

Then the Devil nodded wisely because he's the Devil and he knows the way of these things. When he told me that my pa was a senator for the state of Georgia, I could have shit a brick – I'd voted for the son-of-a-bitch last year.

There was no way that I could get to Pa in his home because it was like a bunker. I guess he'd made lots of enemies. It would have been best to kill him there. To speak to him and explain who I was. Tell him my history and what he'd done to me. But it was impossible. That's why I shot him in the street. You can always get to politicians in the street. I shouted *Pa* to him as he fell, but I think he was already dead. And I didn't see much because security and police were all over me in a few seconds.

The Devil understood why I did it, even though he wasn't too happy about me being locked up and all. It kinda cuts down my options for killing. I saw him yesterday and do you know what he said to me? Of course, you don't. He said that he was going to fix it so that they had to let me out. He can't afford to have somebody he's spent so long schooling in his ways locked away. He's going to have a quiet word with the jury.

Well, shit me sideways – guess what, Mr Reporter Man? The Devil just appeared in this very cell with us here and now. Tell your readers that! Can you see him, leaning against that wall? Of course, you can't. And it's a good job because he's looking really pissed at me today.

Phew-wee! It's a good thing you can't hear what he's saying as well.

You *want* to know what he's saying? Are you sure?

Okay. He's says that when I get out of here, I'm going to have to kill you. He don't want all this getting in the paper and making it more difficult for me to do my work and all.

Hell, if that ain't breaking news for you, I don't know what is.

You going already? Gonna start writing? That won't do you no good. That article ain't going to see no print. I ain't ever failed to kill somebody when I been asked to. I'm a professional, just like you. That's right – you run home. See you soon, Mr Reporter Man. See you soon.

RETURN OF THE HERO

A horror story in 333 words

He places two hands around the cold pint of Guinness. Savours the chill that seeps into his flesh. Raises the glass to his lips and swallows; ice cold, sliding down his throat, the slightly burnt taste, the taste of home.

Ducks quack and preen on the village pond. The early evening sun is hazy amongst candyfloss clouds. She sneaks up on him. Kisses him on his neck, laughter, her arms gripping him. He's twisting, trying to slide free of the beer garden table, to grab her, to crush her to him so they can be one again. Then she's in his arms, face masked by a spill of unruly blonde curls, her cool soft lips meet his, tears are shared.

"You're home," she says.

The sunlight blinds him. He can't see her face, just that smile; the smile that means *Everything is okay, you're a good man, I love you.*

He's walking up the sloped garden towards the pub to buy her a drink. He doesn't know this pub. Doesn't know why he's meeting her here, not the airport, not at home. He stumbles and is suddenly inside the pub. Loud voices. There's a television on above the bar. A young soldier wearing sand-coloured battle fatigues and a webbed helmet grips a machine gun and yells out of the screen.

He can't hear the words. Why didn't she meet him at the airport? She always meets him at the airport when he returns from a tour. He edges closer to the screen. A man bumps into him, elbows him in the chest.

He falls back, winded, pain flaring. He's on his back and the young soldier is yelling into his face. The pub is gone. He's lying on dirt in a shattered, tan coloured building. Bullets rip through a wooden shutter and puncture the back wall.

He tries to speak, but he can only conjure bubbles of blood. He closes his eyes, smiles, and places two hands around the pint of Guinness.

THE MUTUAL PLEASURES OF
BROTHERS-IN-ARMS

I tell you this for nothing: violence will occur tonight.

No doubt.

End of.

Every fucking Friday night he's here. Occupying the same corner of the pub with his pissed-up mates. Burning off the week's boredom with alcohol, laughter, nicotine and the hope of pulling skirt.

He's here and I hate him. I hate him totally. It's eating me up. I don't know why. It's not as if he's come into *my* pub, invaded *my* local. This is a town pub surrounded by dozens of other town pubs that look the same and sell the same beer, the same double-shots-for-the-price-of-one during a happy hour that lasts half the day.

I neck a Jager. Grimace. I hate Jager. Don't know why I drink it.

Somebody is asking me a question in a tone that means the question is really a joke. I ignore them. Refocus on him. He chugs a shot and pulls a face.

Why do I hate him? It can't be anything to do with what he's doing. I'm doing the same things myself. Pints and chasers. Waving my hand through the hot air as I tell stories to my four drunk and loud mates. Eyeing up the girl in the tight red dress.

I pull my gaze away from the man and give Gerry a rough slap on his flabby jowls. A couple of words of encouragement: "Your round, Fatboy!"

Everybody laughs, even Gerry. His tracksuit top is as snug as the skin on a Cumberland sausage. He squeezes through the crowd surrounding the bar, eyes angled at the girl in the red dress.

When he returns, I start work on the next pint and force myself to indulge them with a few Fatboy jokes. But my attention is drifting away from the group. I can't concentrate on their banter. It's *his* fault. I'm distracted by my hatred. It's worrying. Gnawing. Normally, I'm quite clear about my reasons for wanting to kick somebody's head in.

I stare at him, and what do you know, he's staring straight back at me. God, he's ugly; thin weasel face, bright ginger hair gelled back into an arrowhead widow's peak and a feminine upturned nose.

Ginger. I decide to call him Ginger.

I hold his gaze. I'm good at this. I used to practice on my mum's cat; holding its head in front of me, staring into its big brown eyes, seeing which one of us would blink first. The cat never beat me. After it was pancaked diving under our neighbour's motorhome, my mum accused me of giving it a nervous breakdown. Cats don't top themselves, I told her – not unreasonably, I thought.

Is Ginger sizing me up in the same way I am him? Why does he keep matching my stare? Then it hits me: it's so bloody obvious. The reason I hate him is that *he hates me*. It's so simple. He smiles, as if the same flash of inspiration might have lit up his ginger brain. It's liberating. Legitimising. Now I really want to do him some damage. I need to purge myself of this hatred.

It's my round, so I push my way to the bar, ignoring Red Dress even though she's saying something to me in a sing-song voice, and call over to the barman. I turn around to look at Ginger and... *shit*! He's not there. A group of teenagers move away from the fruit machine and I see him on the far side of the pub, slipping into the gents. My breath quickens. This situation requires action. Before I know what I'm doing, I'm across the pub and following him into the toilets.

I'm at one end of the row of bright urinals, Ginger is at the other. And he's singing. At first, I can't work out what song it is, then I realise that it's an old Blur track that I really like. In fact, it's maybe my favourite song. The floor seems to tilt. I feel dizzy. I don't like coincidences like this. I'm not superstitious, nothing like that. But coincidences are usually bad omens. Right?

He's freaking me out. Should I do it here? Casually walk to the sinks, rinse my hands, swivel and smash his face into the white tiles. Punch him in the kidneys. Kick him in the head. Watch him bleed under these bright strip lights. Red on white. I examine him out of the corner of my eye. I can't see the size of his tool because it's hidden behind one of the lozenge-shaped dividers between the urinals. Understand that this is purely a matter of male curiosity. Nothing more. I decide to make my move, but before I can zip up, he's finished and walking towards me. I tense my body but let one arm dangle free. His shoes squeak on the wet floor. Partial reflection in the gleaming tiles. A small cough. My ears sing in anticipation of a fist in the side of the head.

"Follow me," he says and walks out into the wall of noise.

He's taking the piss!

I count to twenty – *calm down fella* – and walk back into the heat of the lounge. He's standing behind one of his cronies, patting him on the back, joking with the rest of the circle. With a thumbs-up gesture, he walks out into the night. My breath quickens. I follow. Ginger's waiting for me at the entrance to an alley alongside the pub. His face seems different under the neon glow of the pub's sign – fleshy and discoloured.

The cocky bastard beckons me with a crooked finger and disappears into shadow. I'm going to hurt him. I'm *really* going to hurt him. Anger twists my walk into a stuttering skip, I'm bouncing on the balls of my feet. It's pre-violence ballet.

"Are you ready for some?" I say, stopping just beyond an arm's length from him.

He grins at me and stands still. His eyes are unreadable. For a second, I doubt my ability to take him. I give myself a mental slap and step forwards, forcing myself to take the initiative. To my delight, he gives ground.

That's all it needs.

As if in response to a ringside bell audible to me alone, I fly at him with a series of powerful but wild blows. Ginger retaliates. Knuckles slam into flesh. Blows are blocked. We're both searching for a haymaker to make the contest short and bloody, but we're evenly matched. A glancing blow nicks my chin. I ram the flat of my hand into his nose. Blood gushes onto my palm and I feel my pulse surge in response. We scuffle. Move in and out of range. Short breaths. I double up and wheeze as he smashes a knee under my protective arm and into my guts. He grins and crooks a finger again. I spit out a lump of phlegm, then piledrive him into the wall. We grapple, punching ribs and butting heads before flying apart like matching magnetic poles. There's blood dripping from his nose and chin. He looks tired, weak. Again, I launch myself at him. At the last moment, he raises an arm to defend himself and our right hands lock together as if to engage in a handshake. I squeeze hard, trying to grind bone and ligament together. He's squeezing back, hard. Shit, he's got a bionic grip. Sharp splintering pain knifes my hand, and my grip disintegrates. The pain is incredible. Blinding.

"Stop!" I shout, waving my left hand in surrender, but his face is also full of pain and fear and incomprehension. He sees the mirror of emotions on my face and throws himself into a frenzy, dragging me by the hand from wall to wall. I try to let go, to pull my hand free, but his grip is absolute. Through the madness of it all, I realise that the pain in my hand has stopped.

We collapse against the wall in exhaustion. Slide to the floor. I look down at my hand and – *Oh God, Jesus Christ*. I feel like fainting. Ginger sees it at the same time.

"Shit! What's happened?" He jerks and wipes spittle from his chin.

I shake my head. All I know is that where only a matter of moments ago we each possessed a perfectly functioning right hand, we now share a fused lump of scarred flesh. Our hands are melded together like pieces of wax, leaving only hints of our former limbs – a couple of fingernails jutting out at odd angles, fingerprints stretched and distorted into contour maps, the odd knuckle forming a lump. My sweat begins to cool in the night air.

"*Oh shit oh shit oh shit...*" Ginger whimpers, on and on, switching his fevered gaze from the former-hand-now-lump to my face and then back again.

"What're we going to do?" he says.

"Fuck do I know?" I say.

"Hospital?"

"No way," I explode. "I'm not having anybody see me like this. It's not... natural."

"What, then? Where's my hand?" He's shaking his arm violently.

"Stop it. This is your fucking fault, Ginger."

"Don't call me Ginger," he screams. "My hair's not ginger!"

He scrambles onto his knees and throws a weak punch with his left hand. He can't get any leverage because we're too close together. "This is *your* fault. You shouldn't have followed me."

I twist to one side and get an arm around his throat.

"Now listen. We have to sort this out together. Calm the fuck down?"

He says nothing. I tighten my grip.

"Understand?"

This time his answer is halfway between a grunt and a cough. Charitably, I take it to be a yes.

"I've got an idea," I say, but I feel sick even allowing the thought into my head.

I pull him to his feet by our shared limb and drag him down the alley to the shopping square at the far end. My limbs are very tired. Strangely inflexible.

A look of sick resignation spreads over Ginger's face as I smash the window of the gardening shop. An alarm bell clatters. I knock aside a few jagged pieces of glass and lift an axe out of the window display. It's two-handed with a bright new blade, two-thirds red, one-third silver cutting edge. Ginger twitches. I can't believe I'm going to do this. It's going to hurt like a bastard's bastard.

"Oh Jesus, no," he says.

"Have a better idea?" The words come out slurred. My face feels tight.

He stares at the blade, works his jaw. He must be feeling the same sensations as me. Finally, he shakes his head, slowly, as if it's the greatest effort he has ever had to make.

"Just do it," he says, words muffled like he's speaking around stones. He shuffles a couple of steps back so that our shared limb is stretched between us.

It takes an immense effort to raise the axe with my left hand. Slowly, I lower it so that the blade touches the mess that was our hands. My joints are seizing up. I can barely flex my arm. I raise the axe for the cutting stroke.

"Not there," he mumbles. "In... middle. Too close to me."

"Is... middle." Shit, my jaw is locking up.

He tries to point to a spot closer to my body, but his arm isn't responding properly. "That's middle... there... nail sticking up."

"No."

"Yes."

"That... nearly... my... elbow." My tongue feels like a dead eel.

"Tha... alfway."

"Bull...it!"

We're running out of time. I'm doing this my way. I raise the axe above my shoulder, poised for the downward stroke, but my arm stops responding and slowly gravity pulls it and the axe down behind my back. I try to let go of the handle. I can't. My senses are buggered – I can't tell where flesh ends and wood begins.

I feel a distant sensation at my neck. Ginger is trying to strangle me. Except he's no longer ginger – he's grey. His hair is grey and so is his flesh. Even his mouth, open in a wordless scream, is a gritty, stone grey. My right arm is the same colour. And the colour is spreading. *Oh Christ.* I pull away from him, determined to free myself before it's all over. With a grating sound, his hand comes away from my throat and his arm falls slowly towards his body like a counterweight.

I meet his gaze for the last time and try to cast a look of hate into my eyes. I lose all control of my limbs and our rigid, unbalanced bodies topple towards each other.

Our open mouths meet.

A perfect seal.

CHALK BODIES

Spanner Man, Spanner Man
You'd better watch out for Spanner Man
You can stick out your tongue
Or call him names
But if you steal his apples
He'll smash in your brains

The playground rhyme circles through Matthew Cooper's mind. He turns to Stu for reassurance. His friend is a tubby silhouette, pinpricks of moonlight in each eye as he stares through the hedge at the old house beyond. Matthew follows his lead, momentarily closing his eyes to improve his night vision, but a gust of wind flicks branches against his cheek and, panicked, he opens his eyes, brushing the branches away.

"Chill," hisses Stu.

Beyond the hedge, the house's gloomy facade is devoid of light or life.

Stu insisted they come at night, reasoning that it would scarcely have been a dare if they'd broken into the house in the day. Stu has a passion for dares and Stu is Matthew's only friend. What else could Matthew do but agree to this adventure?

Matthew's dad had told them that, in his school days, the house had stood solitary in a field, with only the neighbouring school for company. The school had closed two decades ago, and over the years more and more of the field had been bought and developed by housing companies. Now the old house was surrounded by a new housing estate. Three storeys tall with a curious lopsided design, it had stood like an architectural Canute before a wave of conformity. But finally, its defiance is over and Spanner Man's house is to be demolished within the week.

Matthew jumps when Stu taps him on the shoulder.

"I dare you," says Stu, raising an eyebrow and then pushing his way through the hedge.

———

LAWRENCE COOPER TURNS off his television and eases himself back into his armchair, his back grumbling, sciatic pains shooting down his left leg. Eyes closed, he takes three deep breaths. None of the pap that the television offered as entertainment has distracted him from the fact that it's eleven o'clock and his son isn't home. He checks his mobile. No responses to the string of texts and calls he's made. No doubt Matthew's with Stuart Phillips. That boy is a malign influence, a troublemaker. He reminds Lawrence of himself at a similar age, which is a bad thing.

Lawrence's anxiety is increased because he knows exactly where they are. He should never have told them about Spanner Man. He rests his head in his hands and pushes his knuckles into his eyes. Coloured lights flare on his retina, but they can't obscure his memories.

Spanner Man in his soiled white vest, spying on school-children as he tinkered with his decrepit truck. The blue smudge of his tattooed biceps. His mother, sitting in her wheelchair, always looking down onto the playground from an upstairs window. The headteacher's stentorian warning to keep clear of the house after children had allegedly been threatened. The rumours that the old woman was dead. Then the murders.

Lawrence had been drinking. He'd gotten carried away. He couldn't stop the lie coming out. It had been locked up inside for so long he almost believed it now. Matthew and Stu had sat marble-eyed as he told them about the two boys, Lawrence's friends, who had been killed while stealing apples from Spanner Man's trees. He told them how he'd tried to rescue them, but Spanner Man had knocked him unconscious, and it was only the police arriving that saved him from the same fate. They'd called him a hero in the newspaper, but he didn't feel like one. He'd tried to save his friends but failed. Inside the house, the police found the two dead boys and the body of Spanner Man's mother. He had beaten all three to death with a heavy spanner. Nobody knew why he did it. Lawrence's headteacher had told a shocked assembly that Spanner Man was the embodiment of evil. The true reason for his actions was a secret Spanner Man took to his grave. A week after they arrested him, he hanged himself in his cell.

THE BOYS TUG at the board again, and this time it breaks free of the window. The interior smells of dampness and decay.

"Get in," says Stu. His face twitches with nervous energy.

"You first," says Matthew.

"Chicken." Stu hauls himself through the window and disappears into the gloom. Matthew waits, ears alert for any sound not attributable to his friend. Stu's head and shoulders rise to fill the gap. "Come on then, Captain Capon."

Matthew passes the torch to Stu and scrambles through the opening. Inside is a fantasyland of rot and decay. Paintings with mold-eaten faces. Clouds of dust writhing and twisting in the torch beam. Walls sloughing wallpaper skins. Dense spiderwebs billowing. Plaster board sagging like pregnant bellies. The floor tilts. The room's geometry is askew.

They exit the room and creep into the entrance hallway. Matthew swings the cone of light and finds cupboards long ago looted of their contents and now home to mice and more spiders. The mess of rotten plaster, curling linoleum and filth on the floor crunches beneath their careful tread.

The house's discordant symphony of creaks and groans is just beginning to seem familiar, when a new sound disturbs them. Rusty wheels squeaking as they roll over floorboards? The boys stare at each other. Matthew can senses his pulse in his tongue, his ears, his entire body. The noise stops and the steady rhythm of the house reasserts itself.

"What was that?" Matthew whispers, gripping Stu's arm.

Stu shrugs. It's not a convincing show of insouciant

courage. His voice wavers. "Old houses are noisy. Let's find the chalk bodies."

This is the crux of the dare. Stu reasoned that if the police had found the bodies of the murdered kids in an upstairs room, they should be able to find the chalk outlines of the bodies which the police always used to mark where victims fell.

I AM A LIAR, thinks Lawrence. *A keeper of false narratives.*

Lawrence had been a miner until ill health forced him into early retirement and a life funded by benefits. Every day he'd risked his life deep below the surface, digging out the mysteries of the planet's fossil past to power its future. He lived in the dark with his comrades and did not fear it. But now he has his own solitary pit dug deep into his memory. It is cold and midnight black and at the bottom lies a secret: at the bottom lies betrayal and cowardice. He never wants to visit this pit, but it keeps calling him back, calling him back in a voice that he knows. A voice that belonged to a big man who wore white vests and had tattooed biceps.

HE WAS A SCHOOLBOY, hiding beneath an apple tree edged with moonlight. He twitched, nervous as a mouse, as he kept watch for his friends. They were busily stuffing a satchel with apples. A shadow passed over him. A man. He had to shout out now. He had to warn his friends. But a gag of fear covers his mouth. His flesh petrified. He became a statue in the night. The shadow hefted a large spanner. It slid closer to his giggling friends as they struggled to fasten the bulging satchel. The spanner rose and fell, rose and fell, rose and fell. Savage blows collapsing skulls and extinguishing life. The white vest was wet with blood. It looked black in the moonlight. The shadow dragged their corpses towards the house. Lawrence ran. And the shadow came after him. Undergrowth snatched and snagged and tripped him. Mewling, he scrambled to his feet, hearing the shadow crash through undergrowth. Lawrence sprinted, ignoring branches whipping his face, the brambles clawing shins, ignoring the terror that a meaty hand was about to grab his hair and throw him to the ground, on through the trees and out onto a path. The shadow bellowed with frustration.

LAWRENCE CLAMBERS UP and out of his personal pit. He is gasping for breath. He slaps his face and forces himself to concentrate on the room: lamp, chair, sofa, television, clock.

God, what did I do? He often weeps after a visit to the pit. Tonight is no different.

Why didn't I call out?

Oh God, why didn't I call out?

THE TORCH LEADS them up the stairs. Matthew's ears strain to catch the sound of squeaking wheels. All he hears are old timbers shifting against each other like arthritic bones.

"Top floor," whispers Stu.

They climb again. Matthew has a growing urge to sprint

up the stairs, glance into the bedrooms and then flee the house. He wants the ordeal to be over.

As they reach the top floor, the steady squeak of unoiled wheels echoes up the stairwell. They react in tandem, spinning around and peering over the bannister. The windows on the top floor aren't boarded but the pale gleam of the moon does not penetrate the shifting gloom of the floor below. The squeaking stops.

"Shit," whispers Matthew, rubbing his mouth.

Stu ignores him, stepping back and exploring the landing.

Matthew stays at the bannister, peering down to the first-floor landing. He tries to drive back the darkness with his torch, but the weakness of the beam only creates a theatre of shadows – black flames, serpents, cowled figures and a face with puffy skin the colour of cheese. Matthew nearly drops the torch. He plays the beam back over the doorway where he had seen the face. It's just a scruffy circle painted on wood.

He's had enough. He turns to Stu with a whispered plea to leave forming on his lips, but screams and holds up his arms when he sees the shadow raise the spanner.

"Christ, shut it! What's the matter with you?" hisses Stu.

"The bloody spanner."

"I found it by the wall." Suddenly, Stu seems to realise what he's holding, and he drops it to the floor. It clunks heavily. Stu rubs his hand against his jeans.

"Let's get out of here," says Matthew.

"Chalk bodies first," says Stu. "That's the dare."

Stu disappears into a bedroom. Matthew picks up the spanner. If he's carrying it, nobody else can. The first and second bedrooms are empty. Moonlight licks the flaking walls with pewter light. No chalk bodies.

They enter the remaining room. The room from which Spanner Man's mother watched children cavort around the playground. Thick board seal the windows. Matthew lifts his torch and tries to chase away the darkness. There's somebody sitting in a chair by the window. Suddenly, Stu is running from the room, yelling for Matthew to follow him. But Matthew stands still. There's something about the figure that's affected him. A familiarity of posture. The way it sits with shoulders hunched forwards, hands spread across its knees. The way it sits off-centre as if to relieve a pain.

Torchlight hits the figure. It gleams dully. Matthew realises that this is a statue rather than a person. A life-sized statue carved from some dull white substance. He moves to stand in front of the seated figure and shines the torch directly onto its face. His father's face stares back at him with blank chalk eyes. Matthew's legs buckle and he totters backwards until he finds a wall to lean against. That's why the posture was familiar. It's the body shape his father always assumes when sitting in his favourite armchair.

Matthew moves to one side of the statue, but its blank gaze seems to follow him. He shakes. Why is this here? The statue repulses him. There is something abhorrent about it. It is like his father, but it isn't. It's a likeness fashioned by hate. By lies. It makes his father look weak.

He notices the weight of the spanner in his hand and, without thinking about what he's about to do, he raises it high, smashing it down onto the back of the statue's head. Splinters of chalk explode in every direction. Matthew rubs his face and picks out fragments from his eyes. Through tears he sees bigger pieces of chalk lying by the wall, draped in shadow. They look like lumps of coal.

The spanner slips from his hand, and he flees the room. He bounds down the uneven stairs, bouncing against the bannister. The flights seem endless. His legs are weak. He trips as the ground floor rises to meet his feet. But the house can't stop him now. Back on his feet, he drags himself through the window that he and Stu cleared earlier.

He runs again – ignoring a terrified Stu, who materialises from behind a bush – and keeps on running until he is home.

He pants desperately as he walks up the front path. The downstairs light is on and he knows he's going to be in serious trouble for staying out this long after his curfew. He doesn't mind. His dad's anger will be a blessing after the horrors of the old house.

He lets himself in through the front door. There is no noise from the living room, and he guesses his dad must be reading. He pushes open the door. The only light in the room comes from a small lamp. At first, he thinks his dad is sleeping. He's sitting in his favourite armchair, shoulders hunched forwards, hands on knees. But then he sees bone and blood and brain. A trapped splinter of chalk jabs into Matthew's eye, but he doesn't cry until he hears the tread of heavy footsteps and the squeak of rusty wheels coming from upstairs.

I, SURROGATE

The sand wasn't yet too hot to walk on with bare feet, but the air was already humming with heat. Jimmy Swain sat on the corner of a sun lounger and rubbed his stomach. His ulcer had kept him awake again. As had the calculations with which he'd battled before collapsing into bed. In his dreams, numbers tangled together, multiplying his woes and inadequacies, adding to his guilt, subtracting from his self-esteem. Despair resulted from the dream equation. He'd woken to cold clarity: he'd doomed the family business, unless he swallowed his titanic pride and begged his father for help.

Please Lord, anything but that.

Ten metres from Jimmy, a domed metal cage protected the disturbed sand over a loggerhead turtle's nest. Jimmy had already met the Turtle Patrol, a load of woke students from northern Europe who'd decided it was their calling to ensure the survival of this prehistoric species. Darwin obviously hadn't foreseen the rise of such egotists when he wrote *On the Origin of Species*. They ought to try a proper day's work and let be what will be – survival of the fittest.

After breakfast, Jimmy positioned himself in a shady corner of the open-sided beachfront taverna, took a lung-filling breath to prepare himself, and opened his iPad's email app. Time to write to his father. He stared at the white page and the pulsing cursor. He flexed his fingers. Searched for an opening line. Nothing came. He counted the cursor pulses. When he got to five hundred, he decided he needed some Dutch courage before he could make the leap to setting down words. He waved over a waiter and ordered a bottle of retsina. Nothing too strong this early in the day.

A group of seven newly-arrived tourists entered the taverna accompanied by a uniformed, clipboard-touting holiday rep. To Jimmy's horror, the group included children. How in the Lord's name was he supposed to think with ankle-biters running around all over the place? He listened to the rep regurgitate her weekly spiel: basic health and safety tips with a hard sell for excursions tacked on. When the induction was complete the rep twittered to the bored-looking barman for a few minutes, then *putt-putted* away on a scooter.

As soon as she left, two new arrivals entered the bar. A man and a woman, both dark-haired and milky skinned. Obviously, they had forgotten, or made a conscious decision to avoid, the induction. Their flip-flops grated against the sandy floor as they passed through the bar and out onto the glare of the beach. Jimmy watched them pass. With skin that pale, he was betting on major sunburn by the end of the day. The couple spread towels on the beach and rubbed sunscreen onto their bodies. The woman removed her bikini top and waded into the sea, while the man took stock of his fellow holidaymakers spread around the quiet beach.

Stop looking for distractions, thought Jimmy. *Write the goddamn email.*

He opened a new email template and drafted a message asking his father for a two hundred and fifty thousand pounds, using the most passive-aggressive language he thought stood a chance of success. His ulcer growled at this act of cowardice; this was the man who was primarily responsible for conjuring its bloody presence in his guts, waging a ceaseless campaign for Jimmy to provide him with a grandson – an heir to the family business. Jimmy hated children but, to assuage his father and to ensure the continued flow of family capital, he'd married the first woman who'd have him. As fate would have it, she hadn't been able to conceive a child. However, she he had conceived of methods of spending all his money and then disappearing with his best friend.

THE RHYTHM of night-insect songs soothed Jimmy's mind after the torture of writing and rewriting the email to his father. More retsina also helped. He'd rearranged his supper of grilled octopus a dozen times and used a tentacle to scare a child reckless enough to approach his table, but he'd not so much as nibbled on a sucker. His appetite had deserted him over the past months. He waved at the waiter who unscrewed the cap from another bottle of retsina and brought it to his table, then removed the unfinished food with a heavy sigh.

The couple who'd avoided the induction were on the other side of the taverna, sharing a table with a couple of predictable and depressingly healthy Scandinavians. Jimmy had seen them doing push-ups on the beach earlier on. *Mad dogs and Englishmen? Think again, Mr Coward.*

The dark-haired woman was wearing a short, thin-strapped dress, and even after a day in the sun her skin was still the colour of milk. She was lively and flirtatious, and the Scandinavians appeared embarrassed by what she was saying, glancing at each other with half-hearted smiles.

Jimmy was drunk enough to watch the unfolding drama without inhibition. The looks of discomfort on the Scandinavians' faces were now obvious and, just as Jimmy was considering the feasibility of moving closer to eavesdrop, chair legs scraped against the sandy floor and the Scandinavians, faces red with anger, power-walked out of the taverna.

The dark-haired couple huddled together, whispering, and then abruptly the man stood and left, shaking his head. The woman finished her glass of wine and brushed a lock of hair from her eyes. Without warning, she leant forward and began to cry.

Jimmy didn't know why he decided to try and comfort her. He wasn't adept at dealing with extreme emotions, or any emotions really. Maybe it was the retsina. Whatever it was, he approached her table.

"Are you... err... all right?" he said.

The woman looked up at him and wiped her tears away, smiling grimly. "How embarrassing. Crying in public." She was English.

"Can I... err... get you anything?" Jimmy's chivalrous intervention was petering out into inarticulateness.

"No, thank you. I'm okay, really. Just a silly little row. But that's very sweet of you..." She left the sentence hanging and he realised she was asking his name.

"Jimmy. Jimmy Swain."

"Thank you, Jimmy. My name's Angela." They shook hands, and she held his gaze. "Now, I really must get back and apologise to Antoine. Thank you again."

With that, she left the taverna and disappeared into the shadows surrounding the apartments. Jimmy waved to the barman and asked him to return the grilled octopus.

THE FOLLOWING MORNING, Angela greeted Jimmy as she and Antoine passed through the taverna. Antoine gave him a curt nod. Jimmy watched them strip to their beachwear and then rub sunblock onto each other's bodies. For the first time in half a year, Jimmy felt the heat of sexual attraction. He dragged his gaze away from Angela and started on another draft of the email to his father.

He started drinking earlier than usual. The weather was unbearably hot and the cooling *meltemi* wind promised by the locals had failed to arrive. By early evening, when the insects had formed their nightly orchestra and people were entering the taverna for dinner, Jimmy was solidly drunk.

"Do you mind if we join you?" It was Angela, walking into the taverna from the beach, holding hands with Antoine.

"Of course not," said Jimmy, surprised and a little wary. He waved at the waiter, who trudged across the taverna to deliver another bottle of wine. Antoine wrinkled his nose at the retsina.

They ordered food and chatted. Most of the talk concerned Angela's teaching job. She loved children and had a thousand and one tales to tell. Jimmy nodded and smiled when he thought it was appropriate. Antoine was in technology, but he wasn't inclined to talk about a job he evidently did not enjoy.

When it was Jimmy's turn, he surprised himself. Instead of trotting out one of his well-rehearsed lies, he told them the truth. Maybe it was because he was so drunk, maybe it was the fact that he had decided his only option was to approach his father for help. Whatever the reason, it felt good to release some of the pressure inside him. He was a businessman, an importer of high-quality continental foods for middle-class foodies. But his business was struggling to stay afloat on a stormy sea of debt, coupled with a vicious crosswind of competition. He'd run away to the island of Xantithe to hide from his problems.

Angela and Antoine were silent throughout his revelation, occasionally glancing at each other as if they were sharing thoughts.

"How much money would it take to save your business?" asked Antoine.

"A quarter of a million pounds buys me breathing space," said Jimmy. He'd done the sums often enough.

Angela clutched Antoine's arm. "We can afford that. Go on, tell him. He's a kind man."

"Are you sure?" said Antonine.

Angela nodded.

"Okay," said Antoine, taking a deep breath. "I have that sort of money at my disposal, Jimmy. We could help your business, if you will help us with a problem in return."

Jimmy waded through the shallow waters of his drunken mind, trying to keep up with them. Had he heard Antoine correctly? They were prepared to finance him?

"I don't follow," he said.

"We will give you the money for your business in return for you helping us with a somewhat... delicate matter."

Was this a joke? "Go on."

Antoine took a deep breath. "Angela and I cannot have children."

"I'm sorry to hear that," said Jimmy, looking at Angela. She was wearing a short dress of deep blue. Its thin straps almost looked like veins against her white flesh. Her skin looked cool, soft and welcoming. She was smiling at him.

Antoine looked around the taverna and lowered his voice. "We have tried everything we can, but many techniques are not viable for us. For us to have a child, we need help from somebody else. Genuine help. There is no use for us in messing around with turkey basters or syringes. We have tried that and had no success. Jimmy, we are desperate. As desperate as you are to save your family business. This is serendipity at work." Antoine lowered his voice even further. "What we need is somebody prepared to directly participate in the... sexual act."

Jimmy suspected his jaw was resting on the table, but he was too drunk to be sure.

"We want you to help us," said Antoine.

"We understand many men would not be comfortable with this," said Angela.

Jimmy could smell the flower fragrance of the after-sun cream Angela had rubbed into her skin. Her pale lips were parted in anticipation of his answer. She had a long, smooth neck. He'd almost forgotten the offer of money.

"How do you feel about... you know... sleeping with another man?" Jimmy asked her.

Angela shook her head and smiled. "No, you've misunderstood. I can't have children. You'd have to sleep with Antoine."

"What?" stammered Jimmy. "With Antoine? And how's that going to help you conceive?"

"We're not like other people," said Angela.

"Too bloody right," said Jimmy, standing.

"Jimmy, please wait," she said. "Look at our skin. We're different."

The timbre of Jimmy's voice was indignant. "Too right. You're perverts. I thought there were special resorts for people like you."

"I told you he wouldn't understand," said Antoine, distraught.

"Wait," said Angela. "It doesn't matter what you think of us or our motives, Jimmy, but the money is real. You sleep with my husband and it's yours."

"If I let you play your little perverted game."

"We can wire the money to your account tomorrow morning, can't we, Antoine?" Antoine nodded, but didn't meet Jimmy's eyes. "You can check your account. If it's there..." She didn't complete the sentence.

"Bullshit," said Jimmy, but he was thinking of the money, and whether he could stand to be humiliated at the hands of Antoine, to avoid greater humiliation at the hands of his father. An evening or a lifetime. Indecision set his ulcer burning.

Antoine raised his eyes from the table. "You need our money, Jimmy."

"I suppose you'd want to watch?" he said bitterly.

"I'd like that very much," said Angela.

JIMMY DIDN'T LEAVE his room the following morning. Every half an hour he jumped online and checked his bank balance. He wasn't sure whether he wanted the money to be there or not. At 11.30 a.m. it was: £250,000 sitting in the business account. He stalked downstairs into the taverna. Angela and Antoine were waiting for him.

"Ten o'clock, this evening," said Jimmy, then walked away. He felt simultaneously sick and elated. Just one evening and he could salvage his business reputation with the family and flick a big fat middle-finger at his father. He took a taxi into the local town and slowly got drunk.

The evening was a blur. He went to their apartment at ten o'clock precisely. They were courteous and restrained, and this charade made the evening seem even worse, as if they really believed it was something to do with insemination, rather than paid-for sex.

The bedroom was dark. Jimmy undressed and leant on the bed. Angela said she'd undress if it made him feel more comfortable. Jimmy said he didn't care, just get on with it. Then he felt Antoine's hands on him. The smell of lubricants filled the room, and then Antoine was inside him. Jimmy gripped the edge of the bed. He rocked backwards and forwards. When it was over, he dressed and left without saying a word. He showered several times in his own apartment and drank until he passed out.

———

THE FOLLOWING MORNING, Jimmy packed his bags, took a taxi to the airport and paid way over the odds for a one-way flight to Manchester. He needed physical and mental distance from the events of the previous night. Now that he had the funds, he'd be able to immerse himself in saving his business.

His staff were surprised to see him return early but were elated by the news of the company's financial windfall. When they quizzed him about the details of the deal, he became angry and evasive, and they backed away. Jimmy set to work contacting the suppliers that would save his business and, as expected, they all performed a volte-face at the mention of his improved cash flow.

He didn't return to his flat until late in the evening. His ulcer was burning, and he gulped milk to cool his innards. He showered and fell into bed. But he couldn't sleep. Complimenting his grumbling ulcer was an ache vibrating through his limbs. He dismissed it as nothing more than too much alcohol, stress and... an image of the dark bedroom and the rocking bed strobed in his mind.

When sleep finally took him, it took him with a vengeance, holding him so tight in its grip that he didn't hear his phone's alarm beeping for a while. When he finally stirred, he saw the time, cursed himself and made to roll out of bed. Pain flared across his body, emanating from his stomach, and he was forced to lie still until it receded. *Damn this goddamn ulcer*! He tried to move again, with the same burning results.

Nausea swelled his stomach. Sweat rolled into his eyes, blurring his vision. It was a white blur. Slowly, wincing in pain, he raised a hand to his brow. Instead of sweat, his fingers came away covered in a film of white mucus. *Christ on a stick!* What was happening to him? He needed an ambulance. He tried to move again but his ulcer spewed forth nausea-inducing pain that forced him to remain prone on the bed.

When his body convulsed again, he found himself lying on his side with his head dangling over the side of the bed. Vomit filled his throat, his diaphragm spasming, forcing it upward. He closed his eyes, waiting for the familiar, uncontrollable surge of fluid, but it didn't come. Whatever substance was inside him was too thick for that. Slowly, it filled his mouth and forced his jaws open. He watched as a bright-white substance oozed out of his mouth in a thick, sagging tubular shape about two feet long. He felt like a human tube of toothpaste. It hit the floor with a thump.

Eyes watering, he sucked air into his bruised throat and gazed at the strange sight on the carpet. The lozenge-shaped substance was twisting itself into a new form, squeaking like balloons being contorted into party animals, as arms and legs – at first rudimentary, but recognisable within seconds – began to grow. The gentle swell of a belly appeared. A head forced its way clear of the torso, features forming rapidly, eyes pushing their way to the surface and resting like marbles on bread dough.

Movement between its legs; it was a boy.

It opened its mouth of bright white gums and cried.

Jimmy did not know what hardwired instincts or weapons-grade hormones had been released into his body by the birth, but whatever they were, they overpowered the absurd and horrific events of the preceding seconds with absolute ease. Jimmy reached down and pulled the baby to his chest. He kissed its forehead.

He had a son.

———

THE NEW ARRIVAL – he named his son Jimmy Junior – took up all of Jimmy Senior's time. The following day, he phoned the office and entrusted his shocked deputy with the responsibility for utilising the business' new funds. Then he issued his even more shocked secretary with a long, baby-orientated shopping list. When she asked why, he cut her off with a brisk, "I'm a new man."

Jimmy didn't stop to consider the anatomical significance of what had happened to him, nor did he spare much of a thought for Angela and Antoine. He had a baby to care for, and that was all his body allowed him to focus on.

Necessity being the mother of invention, he started feeding Jimmy Junior with milk issued from a marigold glove with a pinprick in the thumb. Although he realised this method was usually employed when feeding baby animals, Jimmy Junior didn't appear to care as he guzzled with abandon. Half an hour later, he was screaming to be fed again.

Jimmy Senior soon discovered that his son's appetite did not start and end with milk. In the afternoon, as he tried to grab a snack for himself, munching on a biscuit while cradling the baby against his chest, Jimmy Junior snapped out a little hand and quickly devoured the biscuit. Half an hour later, a whole pack of Hobnobs had been consumed. Jimmy Junior emitted a wheaty belch and screamed for more.

Finally, Jimmy Junior fell asleep and Jimmy Senior laid him on the bed. He was contemplating a much-needed doze when the doorbell rang. No doubt it would be his secretary with his consignment of baby para-phernalia.

"Hello," said Angela. Antoine was standing behind her.

"What do you want?" said Jimmy.

"We've come for our baby."

A hormonal wail of protest ran riot through his body, and he clenched his fists. He stared at Angela. "I don't know what you're talking about."

The familiar sound of Jimmy Junior's foghorn cry emanated from the bedroom. He'd developed a worrying snack habit.

"Baby!" said Antoine, pushing past Angela and Jimmy.

"We had a deal. We gave you your money and now we want what's ours."

"But it's my baby, too," said Jimmy indignantly, grabbing Antoine's arm. "I've changed my mind. I can't give him up."

"It's a *boy*?" said Antoine, a note of awe in his voice. "I have a *son*."

Jimmy nodded. Antoine yanked his arm free and sprinted up the stairs to the bedroom. He lifted Jimmy Junior into his arms and immediately the baby stopped crying. Angela put her face close to Jimmy Junior, white skin to white skin, and made cooing noises. He gurgled in reply, reaching for her hair.

"He belongs with us," said Antoine. "He's different to you; we're different to you. You know that."

"But he's my Jimmy Junior." Tears filled Jimmy's eyes. Despite the maelstrom of hormonal confusion urging him to fight for Jimmy Junior, just seeing these strange people together with this strange child, watching Jimmy Junior reacting to their presence... it all seemed so natural.

Antoine was right.

He had to let Jimmy Junior go.

His head dropped to his chest.

"Take good care of him," he said.

Angela kissed Jimmy on the cheek as they left. "We like the name Jimmy. We're going to keep it," she said.

"Thank you," he said.

HIS SECRETARY DELIVERED his order of baby food, bottles, toys and other paraphernalia later that day. Jimmy set them out in the apartment just the way he would have done if Jimmy Junior were still there. He removed the mucus-stained sheets from the bed, stuffed them into the washing machine, then lay on his bed for an hour, crying. He'd have to sell the business now. His loss would always taint it. He sat on the edge of his bed, rocking his gleaming new pram, talking to an imaginary Jimmy Junior about what he should do with his life. Decision made, he opened his laptop and booked a round-the-world flight ticket. Suddenly, the world seemed a much bigger, brighter and more interesting place.

SPEAKING, WHISPERING REALLY

A horror story in 333 words

So, as I was saying before you punched me, it doesn't matter what you believe, it just matters what's what. What's true.

Don't shake your head at me – that isn't going to encourage cooperation, is it?

Okay, calmed down, Inspector? Ready to listen? Then begin again, I shall.

Why did I do it? Because she told me to do it.

Who? *Her.* I don't know who she is. It wasn't a job interview. I didn't apply.

I saw her in the mirror for the first time. A mirror, just like the one behind you. Messy bugger she was. Facing away from me. Couldn't see anything of her face on account of her long hair. She was speaking, whispering really.

Who to?

To whom?

Whatever.

Someone out of view. I pressed my face to the mirror and tried to look into the room – that's what it was – a room on the other side of the mirror. Big mistake. She grabbed me before I knew what was happening. My face half in and out the mirror like it was water. I was drowning, drinking mercury.

She told me what I had to do. Said it was mandatory. A form of calling.

I pledged obedience as she held me and then ran. I thought I could escape her. Went home and locked myself in. But she was there in every mirror. In that room. She had me wherever I ran.

I bought the knife. Rode the escalator down into the tube. Got off at London

Bridge and stared up at the Shard. I thought it was appropriate. It looks like a shank threatening the sky, don't you think? Anyway, this bloke in a suit looked at me funny. He was the one. Knew it just like that. So, I stabbed him and he died. Your men arrested me and here I am.

In front of you. And the mirror. I can see her face peering into the room, speaking, whispering really. She looks just like me.

AFTERWORD

GET A FREE COMPLETE NOVEL, AWARD-WINNING SHORT STORY & EXCLUSIVE DEATHLINGS SHORT STORY

Building a relationship with my readers is the very best thing about writing. I occasionally send newsletters with details on new releases, special offers, and other bits of news relating to my books.

And if you sign up to my Reader Group, I'll send you all this free stuff:

1. A free copy of Book 1 in the Deathlings Chronicles: **All The Dead Things** (averages 4.5 out of 5 stars and RRP $3.99)

1. A copy of one of my favourite short stories, **Manny and the Monkeys** (a blackly comic

horror story that won the **British Fantasy Society Short Story Competition**).

1. A new Deathlings Short Story – **Interview with a Deathling**. Exclusive to my mailing list – you can't get this anywhere else.

To receive the novel and two short stories, for free, just **CLICK HERE**

LEAVE A REVIEW

Enjoy this book? You can make a big difference.

Reviews are the most powerful tools in my arsenal for getting attention for my books. Much as I'd like to, I don't have the financial muscle of a New York or London publisher. I can't take out full-page ads in the newspapers or put posters on the subway.

(Not yet, anyway.)

But I do have something much more powerful and effective than that, and it's something that those publishers would kill to get their hands on.

A committed and loyal bunch of readers.

Honest reviews of my books help bring them to the attention of other readers.

If you have enjoyed this book, I would be very grateful if you could spend just five minutes leaving a review (it can be as short as you like) on the book's Amazon page.

Thank you very much.

ABOUT THE AUTHOR

Simon Paul Woodward is the author of the **Wearing Horror Short Story Collections**, **Deathlings Chronicles** series and **Dead Weapons**.

He makes his online home at www.simonpaulwoodward.com.

You can connect with Simon on Facebook at www.facebook.com/simonpaulwoodwardauthor.

Or via Instagram at
https://www.instagram.com/simonpaulwoodward/

and send him an email at simonpaulwoodward@icloud.com if the mood strikes you.

ALSO BY SIMON PAUL WOODWARD

WEARING SKIN: Wearing Horror Collection Book 1

None of us are what we seem to be on the outside. We are all pretending. We are all wearing skin.

The Angel of Loughborough Junctions: An amoral filmmaker experiences the horror of the world through an angel's eyes.

Children of Ink: A living tattoo breaks one of the Five Laws of Ink and suffers the terror of life away from flesh.

Wearing Skin: Bigotry conquers true love in a blood-splattered tale of body swapping, sex and immortality.

American Sexual Lobster: A seafood chef loses his mind and body on a night of shellfish slaughter.

Manny & the Monkeys: An egotistical writer's life is ripped apart by escalating, and increasingly bizarre, coincidences.

Available on Amazon in Paperback and for Kindle

ALL THE DEAD THINGS: Deathlings Chronicles Book 1

A boy on the run. A dead girl leading a rebellion. Time is running out to save the world of the living.

The deathlings believe Stan is the Seer, a human destined to be their doom. They'll stop at nothing in their pursuit of him, even breaking time itself. Now Stan must find his way to the truth, before the deathlings steal his soul. If he fails, they'll destroy the balance between the worlds of the living and the dead forever.

Available on Amazon in <u>Paperback</u> and for <u>Kindle</u>

ALL THE DEAD SEAS: Deathlings Chronicles Book 2

Pirates rising from the grave. A Cornish village that may not survive the night. A boy fighting to save his dead sister's soul.

Tom blames himself for his sister's death. When he returns to Little Sickle, the village where she died, he's shocked to learn that her soul is still imprisoned there. Now he has one night to face his guilt, uncover the village's wicked past and rescue her from a crew of bloodthirsty, deathling pirates. Damnation or redemption will be his by dawn.

Available on Amazon in <u>Paperback</u> and for <u>Kindle</u>

DEAD WEAPONS: a standalone YA science-fiction thriller

A young man framed for murder. Cyborg black-ops soldiers. A race to save a missing father.

Ciaran agrees to do one last job for this gangster brother. Delivering an AI-powered gun, stolen from a covert government agency, to an underworld boss. As payment, he learns their soldier father's death was faked. When the job goes wrong, he's framed for murder and forced to flee the police, gangsters and cyborg black-ops soldiers. As his pursuers close in, Ciaran discovers a link between his father's disappearance and the covert agency. Now it's a race against time to stop their plans and save his father from a fate far worse than death.

Available on Amazon in <u>Paperback</u> and for <u>Kindle</u>

ACKNOWLEDGMENTS

Firstly, thank you to my readers, your support is truly appreciated. Secondly, thank you to my super-readers, particularly those who got behind the first book in this series including: Tom Dale, Nick Evans, Steve Doyle, Amy Alexander, Joan Russell, Simon Rushton, Tom Farnworth and the wonderful members of the Bookstagram community who rallied to the cause: Dylan Butcher, Elizabeth Suggs, Kebbie Stephenson, xoo_Mandy, Samantha (@Bound & Tagged) and Panayiotis Antoniades amongst others.

Once again, very big thanks go to my brilliant editor Tim Major, who ruthlessly corrected and polished the text, and Stuart Bache for the stunning cover design.

As always, huge love and thanks to my wife, Tracy, for being there for me.

www.simonpaulwoodward.com

Printed in Great Britain
by Amazon